D0853287

Jasmine and Maddie

Jasmine and Maddie

CHRISTINE PAKKALA

BOYDS MILLS PRESS

An Imprint of Highlights * Honesdale, Pennsylvania

This is a work of fiction. Names, characters, places, and incidents are products of the author's imagination or are used fictitiously. Any resemblance to actual events, locales, or persons, living or dead, is entirely coincidental.

Boyds Mills Press
An Imprint of Highlights
815 Church Street
Honesdale, Pennsylvania 18431

Printed in the United States of America
ISBN: 978-1-62091-739-8

Library of Congress Control Number: 2013956268

First edition
The text of this book is set in Centaur MT Std.
10 9 8 7 6 5 4 3 2 1

Design by Robbin Gourley
Production by Margaret Mosomillo

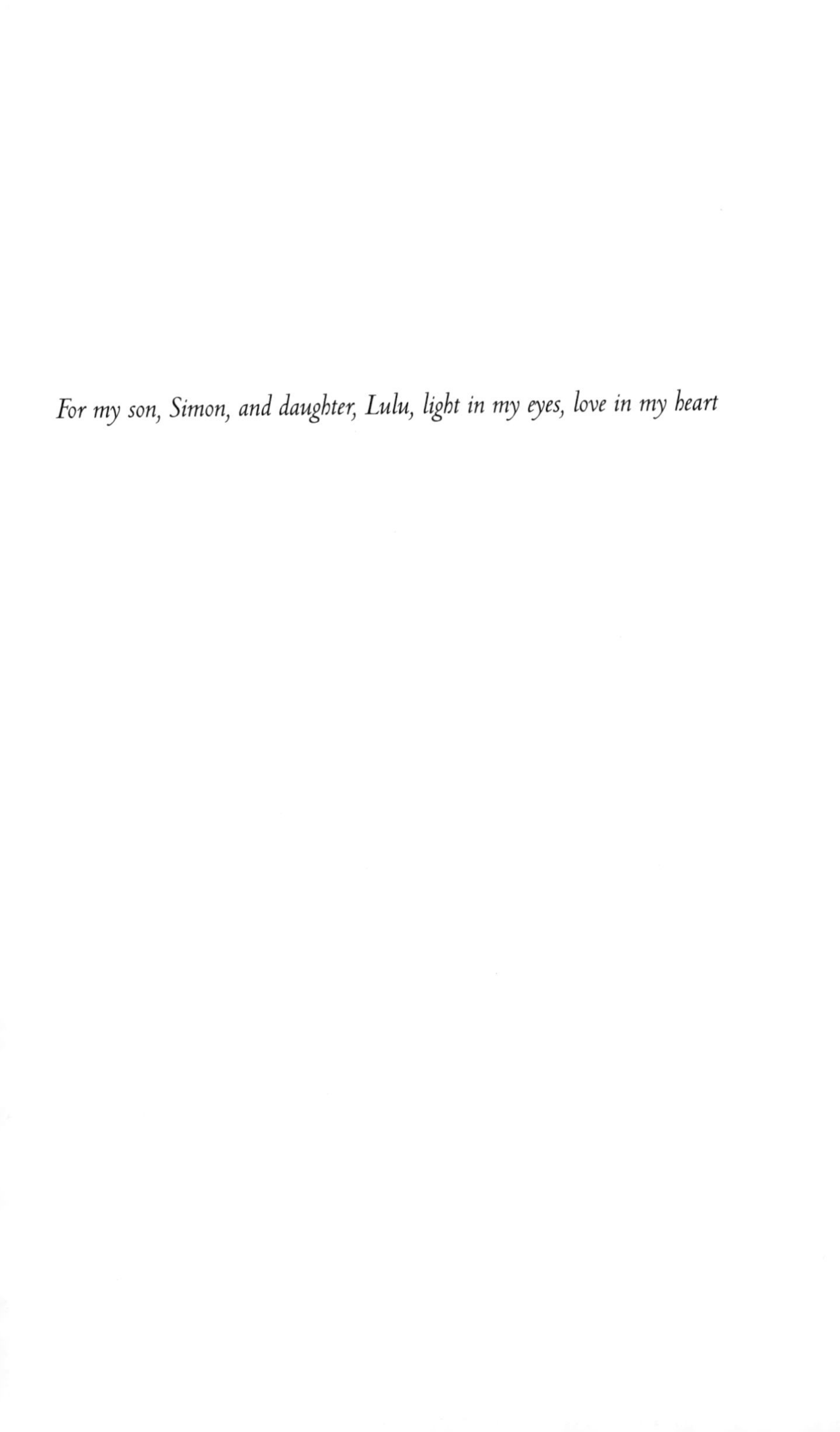

For my son, Simon, and daughter, Lulu, light in my eyes, love in my heart

I'm nobody! Who are you?
Are you nobody, too?

—Emily Dickinson

MONDAY, SEPTEMBER 2

JaSMiNe

First day of school in Clover, Connecticut. We're waiting for the school bus at the entrance to the Wishbone: me, a kindergarten-sized girl, and a tall dude with hair as orange as barbecue potato chips. I have my back to them so I can pretend I'm somewhere else.

The Wishbone. It's shaped just like that—an upside-down Y. We live on the entrance part of the Y, three units in. Each unit is tan, with a small yard in front lined with rhododendrons and boxwoods. It's not the worst place in the world, the Wishbone. That's what I tell myself.

The salty smell of peanut butter wafts over, cutting through the moist morning air. I turn to see why. She holds open her lunch box so he can see inside: white sandwich oozing jelly, chocolate chip cookies, a small peach, a tiny blue thermos. Her cheeks and nose, blotchy pink. Eyes brimming with tears.

"Hand them over," he says matter-of-factly. I stare at his hand, extended. It's huge. He looks about my age, but he's miles taller, awkwardly long-legged, like a newborn giraffe.

"Please, Ian," she whimpers, tilting her blond head up toward him. "Don't take my cookies."

I tell myself to mind my own business. *It's a fresh start,* Mom said this morning, cupping my chin and squeezing one notch beyond comfortable. *For both of us.* Drove off in Ladybug, when it was still dark, to her first job.

Mom's eyes never used to puff underneath, like wells for unshed tears. So I will behave. I will not claw his face, even though I grew my nails for just this kind of emergency.

"Gimme those," Ian says. His buzzed orange hair sparkles. I'm holding in all the breath I own, clenching my fists so tightly the prongs on my turquoise ring dig into my palm. My heart is jackhammering and everything is white around the edges.

Be good, Jas. Be good. Put your best face to the world.

The little blond girl shakes her head. "They're mine."

"Give it." Ian grabs her little arm and squeezes. She holds the lunch box out to him and I lunge for it, snatching it before he can. I close it, clasping the little metal tab. His mouth drops open.

"Seriously?" he says. He takes a step closer to me. "Hand it over."

"Forget it," I spit out. I look straight up at him and notice his eyes, so dark blue they almost look black, especially under his reddish eyebrows.

"Are you going to take my whole lunch?" the girl asks me.

I shake my head. Thrust the lunch box into her hands. "Go stand right there." I point at a spot a few feet from Ian.

She moves to the spot. Her eyes are wide and they dart back and forth between me and this kid.

"Why don't you mind your own business?" Ian says.

"Because I don't like seeing teenagers stealing cookies from kindergarteners."

He flushes, and his dark eyes bore into mine. "You don't even know what you're talking about."

"It's okay, Ian," the little girl calls. "You can have them."

"No, he can't," I yell at her. "Stick up for yourself."

A lady slows down as she drives past in a red convertible. Is she trying to get a good look at the trailer park kids? I flip her off.

The school bus pulls up, its doors squealing open. As I climb on board, I see vacant seats. We must be the first stop, and I'm glad about that.

Ian sits in the last row, apparently too dumb to realize you feel bumps the most back there. I figured that out quickly, after Dad stopped giving me rides to school.

"Will you sit with me?" the little blond girl asks.

"Right behind the driver?"

She pats the seat. Shrugging, I scoot in next to her, and she smiles at me with gapped teeth. Her tears are all dried up.

"Why were you going to let him take your cookies?"

She shrugs. "He just does. He's my brother."

"Your brother?" Stupid-me pause. "Why don't you tell your mom?"

She shakes her braided blond head. "My mom went to Seattle. That's near the Specific Ocean."

"I'm sorry about your mom," I say, casting a glance over my shoulder at Ian in the back row. He mouths a curse, and I mouth it right back at him. Feel a thrum of satisfaction at his surprised eyebrow flick. Turn forward, angry that I felt sorry for him.

"I never remembered my mom," she tells me. Then she holds up her lunch box. "Want one of my cookies?"

"Don't give your food away." It snaps out, that sentence, like a wet towel.

She shrinks back a bit.

I force a little smile to my lips. Didn't mean to scare the kid. "Just some free advice," I add.

The bus turns a corner and she lurches into me. I smell her little-kid smell—breath that doesn't ever stink, soap, a faint whiff of milk. I push her upright, gently, so as not to scare her.

"Where's your lunch?" she asks. One of her hands holds the other hand. She looks like a tiny librarian, a grandma, a little mother.

"I'm going to get it at school," I tell her.

"What's your name?"

"Jasmine. What's yours?"

"Breanna."

She loses interest, I guess, and stares out the window. The school bus turns off Post Road onto a residential street lined with two-story houses.

"Look at that castle," Breanna says. She's pointing at a house on a small side street. It has fancy turrets—I think that's what they're called—on the roof. It's surrounded by a low stone wall wrapped with ivy, and a circular drive swoops up to a wide front porch with a yellow wooden porch swing. I stare and stare, trying to fathom the size of that house. In Rocky Hill, New Hampshire, it would be a Days Inn.

We pull up to the second stop, not far from the giant house. A few boys climb on board, the bus doors sigh shut, and the bus groans away. A girl about my age comes flying out the castle-house's door, followed by her dad, who's holding her backpack. She sprints and hollers, but it's no use.

I stare out the window, watching her as long as I can. Her dad wraps his arm around her slumped shoulders. I've never lived in a house that big. Never even been inside one. But I know what that feels like, to have your dad's arm around your shoulders, that quick squeeze like a jump start to your heart.

She missed the bus. But her dad will give her a ride.

"She always missed it last year," Breanna says, and I realize I'd spoken my thoughts aloud.

When we pull up to the elementary school, Breanna leaps up, then turns back.

"I ate his Hershey's bar," she says.

"What?"

"That's why he was mad and tried to take my cookies."

Breanna hurries off the bus and we rumble on to Clover Middle School, just a soccer field away.

Maddie

I miss the bus this morning. It's a brand-new year and another chance to be a different person. What do I do? I screw it up.

Dad gives me a hug, saying, "Don't worry, I'll give you a ride," in full view of the kids on the school bus—like I'm a little baby, like it's not my last freaking year in middle school.

Here comes the *however*: On the drive to school, he says, "You're too old for this, Maddie. You need to take responsibility for your life."

I stare down at my hands, knowing that Mom told Dad to say that last bit, so that they would be "on the same parenting page."

"Have a great first day," Dad says cheerfully.

I pass by the seventh-grade wing, a twinge between my ribs. Is anyone else like me, always looking back, wishing for something that already went by?

Kate is talking to Aaliyah in the eighth-grade hallway. When I edge up and say hi, Kate waves but keeps talking. It has to do with soccer.

I let myself remember last Friday:

Coach reading the names alphabetically. If you heard your name, you were on the team. *Larson, Menendez, Miller*. The alphabetical list marched on like a Fourth of July parade, leaving me, McPherson, on the sidelines. I turned to look at Kate, sitting next to me, tears shining in her eyes. "Oh, Maddie," she'd said. "I'm so sorry."

The grass under my legs, the bleached blue sky overhead,

the thick, slow realization that Coach didn't call my name. . . .

My face was tight, so tight I could barely nod. When Mr. Miller came to pick us up, I told Kate I would just walk home. The tears began to fall on the way. After they finally stopped, I wiped the tears away, and when I arrived home, I got lucky. Dad was trying to calm down Scooter, who had burned his hand on a cookie tray. He didn't even notice that my life had just ended. Then Lexi got into a fender bender during her driving lesson, and Mom had a migraine from a nasty client. No one remembered that it was the last day of tryouts. Small mercy.

Even if I wasn't the greatest player, I've always been on a team, all these years. Team photo, obligatory brass-colored trophy. Now I'm not on a team, and I'm wondering—who am I? What am I going to do with all this extra time?

As I stand here shifting from one foot to the other, Kate and Aaliyah discuss after-school plans: practice. Practice and more practice. Every day, plus games and practice on the weekends. Bye-bye, Kate. Hello, Discovery Channel.

"My dad will pick you up," Kate says to Aaliyah.

"K." Aaliyah high-fives her and spins away.

"Want to hang out after your practice?" I sound so needy—ugh.

Kate turns to me. "Really? It might be kind of late . . ."

"Never mind."

"Maybe this weekend," she says with a wide Kate grin. "After my game on Saturday."

I feel a coma coming on. A Rip Van Winkle coma that will put me to sleep for about ten lovely years. When I awake, soccer will be no more.

Jasmine

I'm supposed to report directly to the principal's office. The school is humongous, probably twice the size of my school in Rocky Hill. But I'm good with directions, so I follow the signs, past kids who are laughing and talking, girls who are staring into locker mirrors, boys who are walloping each other with backpacks. At the main office, the administrative assistant asks my name, then presses the intercom, murmurs something, and points me to a door down a narrow corridor. I rub my hands on my jeans, wishing I didn't have to be here. Rub my thumb across the indentation my turquoise ring made on my palm. *Put your best face to the world, Jas.*

The door is decorated with a brass plaque that says *Principal Leoni.* When I knock, a rough female voice tells me to come in, so I open the door. It feels like the heaviest thing in the world. But the room smells like apples, and the lady behind the desk is biting into a big red McIntosh.

"Come on in," she says. "I won't bite." Her face is full of freckles, like a little kid's. If she smiled with a mouth full of braces, I wouldn't be surprised. "Help yourself." She points to a huge bowl of apples on her desk. "What's your favorite? McIntosh? Granny Smith? Golden Delicious?"

"No, thanks," I say, as politely as I can.

She cocks one bushy brow. "Aw, come on," she says. "Everybody likes apples, right? Ah, Golden Delicious. Good choice. Take a load off." She points to the plush purple armchair pulled up to her desk. I let my backpack fall to the floor and sit down. Take a tiny bite of the apple, a bigger bite. She smiles at me. "Jasmine Princeton. That's such a pretty name."

A smile tugs at my lips. "I think my grandma changed it to Princeton because of the school. She thought it made our family sound smart." Why am I telling this lady my life story?

"Oh. So you could have ended up Jasmine Einstein?"

And I laugh. "Yeah, I guess."

"You and your mom moved here from New Hampshire."

Blinking fast, I nod. She doesn't say anything about Chelsea, but she must know. To give my mouth something to do, I bite into the apple. It's juicy and sweet, so I demolish the rest, down to the core. Ms. Leoni eats her apple, too; there's nothing but the sound of crunching for a while.

She sets her apple core down. "Mmm, that was good. Well, it's not easy moving, is it?" Before I can answer, she says, "I had to do it in middle school, too. Not fun."

I flinch. Is she going to ask me about Dad? I take another bite of the apple because I don't know what to say.

"It takes a brave kid to do that," Ms. Leoni says, looking at me intently. "I know you lost your dad." She pauses. I grit my teeth against that word, *lost*. But I say nothing. What does she want me to say? I'm not about to discuss my dad with her.

Why do they call someone a *perfect stranger*? Because people seem perfect before they open their mouths?

She picks up again. "It's not fair. Not fair that you and your mom lost him. "

"We didn't *lose* him. He died."

Nodding, Ms. Leoni makes a bridge of her fingers. She studies them for a few long seconds.

"You have every right to be angry," she says. "And it's okay to be angry. As long as you use it the right way. To solve problems. Change the world. Not to do violence on others. Because that doesn't solve anything, does it?"

Oh great. I have Gandhi for my principal. "No, ma'am."

She and I share a look. Somehow I think she knows both my thoughts and my words. She pushes back her chair and stands up. "Well, I don't want to hold you up any longer. Welcome to Clover, Connecticut. I'm going to walk you to your first period—let's see, it's Language Arts with Mr. Carty—and let you get your day started."

We stride together down the hallway, my boots thunking, her heels clicking on the tiles. I pull a tube of lip gloss from my pocket and swipe it across my lips, fake strawberry erasing the faint taste of apple.

Ms. Leoni knocks and opens the door, and I feel like I did the time I jumped out of our backyard maple tree on a dare. The thrill of falling, and the sickness of it, too.

Maddie

"Maddie," Mr. Carty says.

I snap to attention. "Yes?"

Somebody snickers.

A girl in front of me is waving around a sheaf of handouts. I take one and pass the rest to the kid behind me.

"Read page one, which is about course requirements, sign it, and then fill out page two," Mr. Carty says. "Bring it up to my desk, take a copy of the book, and start reading." He points to a stack.

First page: reading, tests, quizzes, participation, blah, blah, blah. Second page: student questionnaire.

Name: I scrawl *Maddie McPherson.*

Occupation: Famous poet. Ha ha. *Student.*

Favorite thing to do: Easy. *Hang out with my BFF.*

Least favorite thing to do: Easy. *Math.*

If you could travel back in time to any era, which would it be? There's the twinge between my ribs. *Third grade.*

Because? *Life was simple.*

Finished, I bring my handout up to Mr. Carty. I'm the first person. I'm not sure if that's a good thing or a bad thing.

"You keep the first page," he says. "And sign the bottom."

I blush and sign, and he rips the stapled papers apart, scans the second page. He nods slowly, then points to the stack of books. "Start reading," he whispers, and I nod. He already told us that, but because I spaced out, and because I forgot to sign my name, he thinks I don't know anything.

I sit down with *100 American Poems.* I love poetry, thanks to Gram. I open up to the first page and begin the introduction. But I don't like introductions. *The history of American poetry is a short one, yet marked by original voices, revolutionary techniques . . . blah blah blah. . . .*

Brendan. . . . What's taking him so long to fill out his questionnaire? Is he writing his life story? Brendan. . . . He got so tall over the summer. I'm sitting kitty-corner behind him. From this angle I can see the gap in his left eyebrow where his brother accidentally hit him with a hockey stick.

He told me that little factoid last year at his Bar Mitzvah. Also that his parents were getting divorced and did I want to go to the Yankee Doodle Fair in June? We went, but Mom saw a text to Kate that Brendan and I hooked up on the Ferris wheel. Mom freaked, even though I explained that "hooking up" didn't mean what she thought. It was just a kiss. Mom saw right through that "just." That I felt the kiss not only on my lips, but in my wrists and knees and toes. No more anything with Brendan. Not until high school.

Too bad for Mom that Brendan and I are in the same English class. And math. And gym.

He looks up and smiles. One of his front teeth has a bright white fleck. I smile back, glance away as casually as I can, over to Kate. She's sneaking Mia Hamm's biography. Alert the newspapers.

The classroom door opens. Our principal, Ms. Leoni, walks in with a girl. Ms. Leoni smells like she took a bath in perfume. Or is it the girl? Mr. Carty and Ms. Leoni whisper to each other for a few moments while the new girl looks at her fingernails. Behind me, Jeremy Rogers whistles. Matt Clemens, across the room, calls out, "Wow."

They notice that the new girl is gorgeous, but I notice her boots first: tall black lace-up boots. Cool. Black boots and long, near-black hair; deep-brown eyes that camouflage her pupils. She has a pink chicken pox scar, directly centered between her thick brows, like an Indian *bindi.*

"Class, this is Jasmine Princeton," Ms. Leoni says.

I laugh.

Ms. Leoni and Mr. Carty glare at me. Brendan raises an eyebrow, and Sarah and Mikayla mouth "OMG." I slink down in my chair and mutter "Sorry," and everyone stares at me for four hundred horrible seconds.

Why I laughed: When I was little, I used to give my stuffed animals fancy names like Wanda La Donna and Francesca de Riche. Jasmine Princeton sounds like one of those made-up fancy names.

But I obviously can't explain any of that to Ms. Leoni.

"Maddie, perhaps you would like to give Jasmine a tour of our school on your way to lunch?" Ms. Leoni asks. Only it's not a question. It's an icy command.

"Okay," I manage.

Jasmine doesn't look too happy about it, either.

"Jasmine, welcome to eighth-grade Language Arts," Mr. Carty says. He hands her the syllabus/questionnaire.

"Thank you," Jasmine says. Ms. Leoni leaves and Mr. Carty blares at us, "Finish up these questionnaires, people. This is not an all-period activity. Jasmine, there's an open desk over there"—he points to one directly in front of me—"or over there," and he indicates the desk behind Kate.

In the front row, Mikayla and Sarah raise their hands. "There's a seat over here," Mikayla says, smiling widely. Sarah pats the back of the seat.

Please, please, sit next to me. I cross my fingers, hope to die, stick a needle in my eye. The minute she sits down I'll tell her how idiotic I was to laugh. Then she'll like me.

Please. Sit. Next. To. Me.

JaSMiNe

I'm about to smile like Mom told me I should. Put my best face to the world like Dad told me in the hospital. Then, I hear it: a laugh. A laugh like a slap.

The girl claps her hand over her mouth, and I know her right away. Smooth light-brown hair and wide-spaced green eyes and a tiny sprinkle of freckles across her nose. Looks like a girl on a "Got Milk?" commercial. The girl who missed the bus.

The smile slides off my lips. Ms. Leoni tenses up next to me like my dog Indy used to do when he saw our neighbor's cat. I twirl the turquoise ring to face in, and squeeze my fist. The prongs hurt, but not as much as that laugh.

No, I don't want a tour. Not with her. Please, no. I blink

hard, hoping that the mascara I stole out of Mom's makeup bag doesn't smear. These kids stare at me, watching, as if they're waiting for me to burst out singing or tap-dancing. I plaster on a fake smile. I make myself say stupid words about being happy to be here.

"Jasmine, there's an open desk over there"—my new teacher points to one directly in front of the girl who laughed. She smiles at me like she didn't just laugh. What kind of game is that? "Or over there."

I follow the direction of his finger and see an empty desk right behind the only kid in the class who's not staring at me. She's got crazy-curly hair. I decide to sit near her. On my way to the empty desk, an Asian girl with black hair shining like a crow's wing smiles at me. The girl next to her, dark brown hair pulled into a high ponytail, smiles too. "There's a seat over here," the ponytail girl says.

I smile and whisper, "I'm not the front-row type," as I walk past, my eyes on the empty seat by the oblivious blond girl.

"Hi," I say. But she doesn't even look up. I step over her feet sticking into the aisle and take my seat behind her. She has a piece of grass in her hair, but I'm not about to tell her.

I read the course requirements, fill out the questionnaire. Another era I'd like to travel to? Random answer: *The French Revolution.* Truth: One year and three months ago.

Last to turn the paper in, I grab the remaining paperback, and even before I can settle into my seat, Mr. Carty says, "Please read up to page ten tonight and be ready to talk about some of the poems you've read. One is by Emily Dickinson."

Mr. Carty talks a bit about Emily Dickinson's life. I hear: Amherst, Massachusetts; recluse; wore white; wrote 1,800 poems. Mr. Carty reads us one of her poems about wild nights. Sounds like it was wishful thinking on her part. But he tells us we can hear the "raw emotion" in her poem. Raw emotion, he tells us, is at the heart of every great poem.

"We're moving on to Writers' Workshop now," he says. He walks around the room, tossing a marbled notebook on each desk. "Meet your poetry journal, my gift to you. Don't lose it. You'll be writing in it a minimum of every day for two weeks, a maximum of the rest of your life."

Someone groans loudly.

"The journal is ten percent of your grade. Another ten percent is participation in the Poetry Café. September 16, in the library. Everyone will choose a poem from said journal and read it."

"Out loud?" Mikayla asks in a horrified voice.

"Precisely." Mr. Carty slings a journal at me. "Don't lose it," he reminds us.

I want to say something back. Like: "Okay if I throw it out? Or set it on fire?"

"Now, people," he says, leaning against his desk. "Find a pen, crack it open, and write 'Someone I admire' at the top of the page."

Someone I admire? I stare at the blank paper, the faint blue lines like railroad tracks running straight off the page. I fold my arms across my chest and hug myself; I cross my legs, too. I want to curl up like a snail.

Someone I admire?

Maddie

He writes on the board: *Write a free verse poem about somebody you admire. No clichés allowed upon pain of my breath.*

Free verse: It doesn't have to rhyme. Ordinary speech can be turned into a free verse poem. Even my grocery list can be a free verse poem.

"Listen up," he says:

I admire my great-aunt
Florence who is ninety-
Six years old and still
Takes the stairs, stays
Up late watching comedy,
Cooks a mean
Chili con carne and loves
Pro wrestling.
If only great-aunt Florence
Would let me drive
Her Porsche.

We all burst out laughing.

Mr. Carty smiles and says, "If I can do it, so can you."

Before I begin, Jeremy taps my shoulder and whispers,

"Do you think it has to rhyme?"

"No." I point to the board. Jeremy nods and starts chewing the eraser on his pencil. Brendan tosses me a note, which I snatch and open.

M&M,
HELP! WHAT SHOULD I WRITE?
KATE

I think for a minute, let my brain go helium. Write back on the same paper:

Call it "Three Reasons to the Third Power." Then give nine reasons why you love Mia Hamm. Be specific!

I *pssst*-whisper to Brendan and hand him the note. It travels across the room to Kate. She reads it and nods.

And then I write, as if my brain and body have nothing to do with it. As if my heart tells my hand what to do:

Somebody I admire is my sister Lexi I hate
to admit because she wears army clothes & still
glows like a heat lamp & she plans to
save the world & save for college &
Mom & Dad gave her Gram's ring
for her sweet sixteen & I loved Gram
so much & now she's gone except for

the emerald ring & so I guess
that means they love Lexi best &
I can't blame them because she gets
perfect grades in all her
AP classes & she always has twenty
friends sitting on our
front porch filling out Amnesty
postcards &
even though
I admire my sister
I sometimes accidentally
on purpose
hide her army jacket
or accidentally
on purpose
use up her favorite
shampoo.
She is sixteen &
perfect & I am
thirteen & Mom says
wake up, Maddie!
Pay attention!
Maddie, why
can't you
be (More) Like
Lexi?

Jasmine

Someone I admire? I know what I have to do. Sneak onto the page with little letters. Trick myself into thinking I'm not writing anything. For my best-face-to-the-world man. For Dad.

mike princeton

he taught me how
to bait a hook
how to be patient
wait for the sudden pull
of the rainbow trout

to walk without noise
how to blow the elk horn
how to take aim
how to give thanks
for the steak.

to hold the knife
thumb to the dull edge
press it into the wood
shave it to the shape
of a fish

to take care of mom
when she cried herself

to sleep, her black
mascara like paw prints
on her pillow.

to not get lost
change oil
throw a punch
listen to a good story

but he
didn't teach me
how to grow up
without him.

Maddie

The bell rings and we run out the door like greyhounds. The halls are full of noise, full of jostling bodies. Kate's waiting for me but before I can catch up to her, Aaliyah and this girl Rebecca swoop in on either side. Go Fairfield United. My feet grow numb inside my sneakers. I putter to a halt, right in front of a poster inviting kids to join the chess club. And maybe I will.

"Hey," Brendan says. "So, how was France?"

I frown at him, even though I want to smile. If I did smile, it might make him think I've been thinking about him all summer. Which I have.

"It kind of blew. But it was kind of fun, too." My face gets all warm. Why is it that when I use slang, I sound ridiculous, but Lexi always sounds scripted—in a good way?

Brendan nods.

"How about the rest of your summer?" I ask.

He shrugs. "Well, actually, it sucked. It was going to—no matter what. But when your mom called my mom . . ."

I wince. Now I'm fairly certain my entire face will just melt off and slither down my neck. The bell rings as we both duck into Ms. Bonner's algebra class. First she swishes around the desks, handing out syllabi, her tan pants crackling with electricity. A teacher's aide follows, thumping down two-inch-thick Algebra One textbooks. Just the sight of all those unread pages and unsolved problems sends acid straight up my throat. *Gack.* I loathe you, Mom; even though I love you, I loathe you. A thin layer of loathe on top of love. Because I do not belong in this class.

Did Ms. Bonner have a terrible childhood? Who else gives a quiz on the very first day of class?

"Think of it as an assessment," she says as she slides the papers face-down onto our desks. "I want to see what you have retained from Pre-Algebra last year."

When she tells us to turn over the paper, I flip it with sweaty fingers. Numbers do that to me. Speed limit: 35 miles per hour. Bananas: 99 cents a pound. You're grounded for: 30 days. I don't like facing the bald truth of numbers. They can never mean anything except exactly what they do mean.

But there's something worse than a number, and that's

an integer. If I'm calm, I realize an integer is merely a whole number that can be positive, negative, or zero. But at the word *integer,* my mind empties of all rational thought. So it shouldn't be a surprise when the twelve problems turn into dancing fairies. Adding, subtracting, multiplying, and dividing integers. Oh, no. I wild-guess my way through the quiz, which I refuse to call by any other name.

"Now you're going to exchange with another student and we'll grade these in class," she tells us. "Front row, pass to the people behind you. Back row, bring your quizzes to the front."

I pass my quiz to Kate. At least my math-dunceness is not news for her. Brendan hands me his quiz. Ms. Bonner reads the answers. Brendan gets a perfect score; he's amazing at math. Math teachers always give him challenge problems. As for me, I get the "challenged" problems. Mom pushed me into the high math class, when really I belong in regular math—or, perhaps, Maddie math.

"If you missed half or more than half," Ms. Bonner says, "I'd like to conference with you."

Kate hands back my quiz with a wincing smile. I missed half, exactly, but Kate's smiley face with the squiggle mouth makes me feel a little better. Brendan glances at my quiz and raises one eyebrow.

Up at Ms. Bonner's desk, I see it's adorned with framed pictures of standard poodles, their eyes glowing red in their black faces. Lordy, lordy, I'm the only person in the class who bombed the quiz. No, here comes some guy from the back row. It just took him longer to figure it out.

"Class," Ms. Bonner announces right into my ear, "please read the syllabus carefully and then read chapter one in your algebra textbook."

Ms. Bonner reminds the boy and me how to add and subtract positive and negative integers.

"A positive integer represents a move to the right and a negative integer represents a move . . ." She looks at me, waiting for me to fill in the blank.

"To the left?" I guess.

"Correct," she says unsmilingly. "Another way to think about it is *minus a negative* can be thought of as *plus a positive*." She shows us several problems and says, "Maddie, pay attention," even though I'm focusing as hard as I can. "Maddie, eyes on the paper," she says, even though I'm staring right at it.

By the time I return to my seat, everybody else is working on the second or third page of the chapter, and I can picture my night. My life. I'll have grey hair and a cane and I'll thump into an eighth-grade math class.

My eyes roam around the room and collide with Jasmine's. She gives me a look so blankly hateful, I gasp. Flinch and look away.

I have no talent for change.

Before lunch, I head to Jasmine's social studies class. Maybe she lied. Maybe she won't be there and I won't have to take her on this heinous tour that:

1. is going to cut into my thirty-minute lunch period,

rendering it impossible to actually get anything for lunch

a. except a bag of chips

b. or possibly a Granny Smith apple

2. will be torture

a. since she hates me for laughing at her

b. because I will wonder for the quadrillionth time:

Why is it so hard for me to make a single new friend?

But . . . there she is. I thread my way through the rows and stand by her desk, waiting for her to acknowledge that I am a human being. She doesn't.

"Come on." I aim my voice toward steady. "I'll show you all the things you need to know to survive."

Everyone has already been vacuumed out of classrooms and into the hall. Everyone but me and this girl, who takes her time stuffing her binder into her backpack. Maybe I am a ghost. Invisible or insignificant. Just a piece of paper or a crust of baguette.

We walk through an empty hall that smells like baloney and sweat. Her black boots beat time on the tile, but I feel the pounding in my head. My sneakers are silent. "Avoid this one if you can," I say as we pass by the bathroom next to the sixth-grade classrooms. She purses her glossy lips and says nothing.

"So how come you moved to Clover?" I ask.

"My mom got a job here, so we moved. Not that it's any of your business."

Band-Aid-ripping-off-skin ouch. "Listen," I say in front of the Art Smart display. "I'm sorry about laughing at your name." Think: *Shut up, Maddie. Stop while you're only hated.* But do

I? Oh, no. I keep talking. "It was a dumb thing because your name reminds me of the names I used to give my stuffed animals." Think: *Good job, Maddie. Now she looks like she'd spray you with Raid if she had a can handy.*

"I didn't even notice," she says.

Brrr. If words were desserts, hers would be Popsicles. We glance at the main office, the library, and the gym, and we don't say a word.

On our way to the cafeteria, we pass Sarah and Mikayla at their lockers. They're brushing their hair and applying lip gloss before lunch. Slamming the doors shut, they move to either side of Jasmine.

"Welcome to Clover," Sarah says warmly. "When did you move?"

Jasmine flashes an oversized bright-white smile, like a beam of light directed right at them.

"July," she says. "Wow, it was a lot hotter than New Hampshire."

"Oh, poor you," Mikayla says. "Much better weather up there, right?"

Jasmine turns her smile to Mikayla, eyes bright and gaze steady. "Yeah," she says. "But I think I'm going to like winter here. Not so much snow."

"I bet you're a great skier," Sarah says.

"I'm not too bad," Jasmine says. "Everyone in my town can ski. It's kind of a rule if you live in New Hampshire."

"I got my mittens stuck on the tow rope when I was a

little kid," I offer to the conversation.

"My parents have a vacation house in Vermont," Sarah says, ignoring me. "Maybe you could go skiing with us."

"That would be amazing," Jasmine says, her smile—even more dazzling now—igniting smiles all around.

"Hey, why don't you sit with us at lunch?" Mikayla says. "Maddie, your table's pretty full of soccer people, right?"

Yeah, right. "Not at all," I say, for once getting words out of my mouth in a timely fashion. Even wilder: "Actually, I just asked Jasmine if she wanted to have lunch at my table."

Jasmine's gaze swings to me. She knows I'm lying, but it's as if that makes me more interesting than she thought. She cocks her head, raises one dark brow, and it all happens at the speed of light. She turns back to Mikayla. "Thanks. How about tomorrow?"

"Sweet," Mikayla says. Then she whips out her phone and asks Jasmine for all her contact information—cell number, iChat, blood type.

I catch my reflection in the window opposite us. I do exist. I'm not invisible.

At the entrance to the cafeteria, Jasmine claims she has to use the bathroom and says she'll meet me inside. I shrug away the sting of it and scan the crowd for Kate. And there she is, by the juice machine, waiting for me.

"Could you be any later?" she says as we hurry to the deli line.

"I had to give Jasmine a tour before lunch," I say. "Did you *not* hear Ms. Leoni yell at me this morning?"

"Oh, right. I guess I was reading about Mia Hamm."

"Yeah. Thanks for caring. Seriously, if we were on a desert island, and a life raft came along with enough room for you and a soccer ball *or* you and me, I bet you would choose the soccer ball."

"That's completely illogical. I could hold the soccer ball."

"That's not the point."

Kate and I grab two cartons of milk, and Kate smacks herself on the head. "Now I remember that new girl. She couldn't participate in gym, right?"

"Yep. Boots."

"Weird."

We take our trays and thread our way through the cafeteria. As we pass the soccer-girl table, Aaliyah smiles and waves at Kate to sit down. Another girl—whose name, I think, is Olivia—jumps up and gives Kate a quick hug. The food on Kate's tray slides to one side before she rights it. "Hey," Olivia says. "That block yesterday was awesome."

Kate laughs and my heart plummets.

"Sit with us," Aaliyah pleads.

"I can't," Kate says.

"We have to talk about our first game," another girl—Shelby? Colby?—says.

Kate shoots me a look. *Do you mind?* it says, and what can I do?

I tell her to go ahead and I move on, past the band geeks

and the soccer guys (Brendan's sitting there, but with his back to me), past Sarah and Mikayla and a few other girls with interchangeable long, straight hair and bored expressions. I plunk my tray down at the lunch table full of ordinary mortals—Megan (a big girl with a raucous laugh), Rachel (worse soccer player than even me), Emma (perma-blush shy), Sorcha (from Ireland and thinks American girls are "eejits"), and now Jasmine, who arrives just as I do. Not that Jasmine belongs with us.

Jasmine smiles. "Hello, everyone," she says, grabbing a seat, and Emma blinks. I know how she feels—Jasmine's smile looks famous, like she's on TV or in the movies or in one of those ads for whitening strips.

"Hey," I say, noticing that Jasmine has nothing in front of her. "You're supposed to get food."

"I think I might have overdosed on sloppy joes back home."

"There's other stuff," Megan says with a grimace. "Salads."

"I'm not very hungry," Jasmine says with a shrug. "My mom cooked me a ridiculous breakfast."

"Ah, back-to-school pancakes?" I ask.

"Something like that."

As we eat our lunches, we all chat, maybe me more than anyone. But after a while Sarah and Mikayla walk over to our table—which they never did in seventh grade. They whisper something to Jasmine, but we can all hear: there's a party this Saturday night; does Jasmine want to go?

Rachel, Megan, Sorcha, Emma, and I look at each other.

They shrug and get up. But I'm caught, staring at Jasmine. She has that something that makes Sarah and Mikayla buzz around, bouncing insensibly off her light. I want her to smile at me the way she smiles at them. I want to be drawn into her light. Why? I don't even know. . . . But I do know that I don't want to be invisible anymore.

Everyone moves off in different directions—and I stay in my seat, gazing now into a corner of the lunchroom, where the PTA has set up a lost-and-found. I think about all those clothes in there—lost. Air whistling through the sleeves instead of warm bodies.

Jasmine

Ripple of Spanish. On the best day, I'd have a hard time understanding what Señora Altman's trying to ask me as she bends over my desk. But now, with my stomach grumbling, I haven't got a clue.

I didn't go through the lunch line. Didn't get a sloppy joe even though I love sloppy joes. What if I was the only one getting the hot lunch? What if someone figured out I was on the "free and reduced lunch" plan? Tons of kids got free or reduced lunch in Rocky Hill, including me. But we only had one line for lunch, not a panini line and a salad bar line and a hot lunch line. I made an excuse to Maddie and texted Mom from the privacy of a bathroom stall: *Can I get a panini on the free and reduced lunch plan?* But she didn't text me back. She was probably too busy peeling wads of gum from underneath desks and emptying trashcans of half-full Diet Cokes and bagels smeared with cream cheese that slid down the side of the can.

I figured it would be better not to eat anything than to risk it.

"*¿Que haces en la escueula?*" Señora Altman asks. But her back is to us as she taps the whiteboard.

With my finger, I trace a name gouged into the desk, thinking about the janitor who will try to get that mark off. Mom might be doing something like that right this minute.

Cleaning schools isn't anything new to Mom. She'd been head custodian at Bridgewater–Rocky Hill Village School. My best friend Carly's mom was the head lunch lady at the same school. Kai's parents ran an auto body shop. Most kids had two parents who worked.

Most. But not Chelsea Thomas. Her dad was my dad's foreman. Her mom stayed home, where she watched home shopping channels and raised Rhode Island Reds so that Chelsea and her brothers could have fresh eggs for breakfast. After Dad died, her family was super nice to us. Chelsea and her mom took me to the outlet mall and bought me new expensive clothes—stuff my parents couldn't buy—clothes I'm wearing here in Clover, including these boots, which cost more money than Mom makes in a week. They took me skiing, another thing my parents had never been able to afford. Although they rented me skis, I couldn't fit into Chelsea's old ski jacket and pants, so I wore my old winter jacket and jeans. I could tell how embarrassed Chelsea was when they picked me up. I sucked at skiing, but her whole family was kind and gracious.

One night her parents took us out for pizza and ice cream at a place with mini-golf and arcade games. The adults stayed inside, drinking from pitchers of Pepsi or beer. In the middle of mini-golf, I realized I needed to use the bathroom, so I came back inside, went to the ladies room and slipped into one of the stalls. Right then, Chelsea's mom came in with one of her friends. Embarrassed, I kept quiet.

"You can't save the world, Roberta," her friend said.

"I know, I know, and lord knows Chelsea's giving me a hard time about it," Chelsea's mom said. "But I told her I wasn't backing down on this one."

"I still think you can't just up and force kids to be friends," the woman said. "It won't work."

"This girl's got nothing," Chelsea's mom said. "Dad's dead and not even thirty. Mom's a total mess. Just fell apart, you know? If it was Jim, I'd be fine. I'd be stronger than that for my kids."

There was a little more talk, a little more back-and-forth about how Pastor Bob commended Chelsea's mom for her act of charity. Then they left.

I flushed, came out, and turned on the tap, waited until the water was scalding hot before I plunged my hands in. I scrubbed them.

Came out of the bathroom with bright red hands and my mouth shut. I was not going to give anything away. I kept smiling that night and every day and night after that. I took their charity clothes, designer boots, expensive makeup and perfume.

But soon the trouble with Chelsea started. What Chelsea said I did. And did I do it? Steal her bracelet? No. She lent it to me. But when she forgot to ask for it back, I didn't remind her. I was her charity case, so why should I give it back? Anyway, I didn't wear it to school—only tried it on at night in my room. That's all I wanted to do. Pretend I was Chelsea, the girl with everything. Like that girl Maddie, sitting over there, staring out the window. Probably daydreaming about all the stuff she wants—and will get—for Christmas.

I'd pretend I was Chelsea, with her big house, skis, cabin on Lake Winnipesaukee. Mom and sister. Dad. Pretend I was the one doling out the charity. But it didn't make me feel better. I wanted to give the bracelet back, planned to put it in her locker.

Before I could do that, Chelsea and her friends cornered me after school. Made a ring around me. It would have been okay if I had just stayed calm.

"After all me and my mom did for you," she said. "And you turned out to be a dirty little thief."

But I didn't stay calm, did I?

My heart hammered, and everything got white around the edges.

And I did a terrible thing. Beat up Chelsea, split her lip, loosened her tooth. Her friends—there were three of them—screamed at me to stop, but they didn't get in my way. All that rage pouring out of me. . . .

It was wrong. I knew it the second Chelsea fell to the ground and my rage collapsed. I tried to kneel next to her, press my sweatshirt to her mouth, but the other girls shoved me away, shielding Chelsea from me as if I were coming back to finish her off, as if I were a murderer, cold blood in me, different from them in my deepest tissues.

Chelsea's mom didn't press charges. She said we'd been through enough. I guess that was Christian charity. I had to go see Dr. Philby. She tried to make me talk about my feelings, but I didn't see the point in that.

Mom knew we had to get out of there. For my sake and for hers. Everything in Rocky Hill reminded her of Dad. Uncle Louie and Aunt Gail lived in Fairfield, Connecticut. Mom saw the ad on k12jobs.com for an assistant day custodian at Burr Farm Elementary School in Clover, Connecticut, right by Fairfield, and she applied. Got the job—from seven to three—and got another one, too, at the mall from five to nine. We could have stayed with Uncle Louie in Fairfield, but Mom wanted to be independent. So we moved into the Wishbone in Clover a month and a week before school started. For a month and a week I went to work with Mom. I didn't—couldn't—let her out of my sight.

Someday, she says, we might go back to Rocky Hill. We'd move back into 908 Airway, and I'd get Indy from the Grays. I'd weed the garden and get it ready for spring planting.

I lie. She never said we'd go back. Everything else is true.

Maddie

I stand in line, studying the yellow of the school bus. How did they come up with that color? Did they have to pick just the right color to make the bus seem safe and happy even if the kids didn't feel safe and happy getting on it? It couldn't be daisy yellow. That's too springtime. Or fluorescent yellow. Too wild. It couldn't be pale pastel yellow. Too indecisive. It had to be just this kind of yellow, the color of an egg yolk. I think of whole yolks and broken ones and if I think too long, I won't like breakfast anymore.

Someone taps me on the shoulder. A gentle, quick tap. "Hey."

I whirl around. "Hey, Brendan."

Silence. And more silence like a piece of taffy pulled as far as it will go. My throat feels like it's squeezing shut, like I can't swallow. And I can't *not* swallow.

"I can't believe we have to read a poem out loud," he says.

"Yeah." Boy, I'm a brilliant conversationalist. I try desperately to think of something else to say. "Did you like Emily Dickinson's poem?"

He looks puzzled. "Who?"

"The 'Wild Nights' one. The one Mr. Carty read to us," I explain.

"Oh. Uh, it was okay. You?"

Should I lie? I decide not to. "Yep. I love her poetry."

He grins. "Then maybe you can tell me what it's about."

I smile back, thinking, *It's about wild passion, so . . . no way.*

"And you can tell me how to add negative numbers."

Kate bounds toward us, stopping with a jump. She high-fives me, then Brendan. "Dude, you made Fairfield United?"

"Yep," he says. "How about you?"

"Well . . . duh." Kate squints at him, her blond corkscrew curls shimmering under the afternoon sun.

"How about you?" Brendan turns to me.

Soccer. Two syllables that cut like scissors.

"Nope." I heave out the word along with a sigh.

"She had an awesome tryout," Kate informs him. "There were just too many girls trying out."

"Kate . . ."

"That's too bad," he says to us. "There's my bus. See ya."

"Bye," we call out in unison after him.

"I'm not surprised he made the boys' team," Kate says. "He's totally awesome."

The funny thing is, she means that in a soccer way. Not a cute-guy way.

Memory: Brendan in third grade, my second-best friend. Brendan in sixth grade, the star pitcher when Clover made it to the Little League championship, suddenly popular—and out of reach. Then, Brendan in seventh grade, grey-eyed and serious, in Spanish with me. Flunking until I bailed him out. Brendan, listen: *¿Dónde está la tienda de comestibles?*

My bus is next, so I get back in line behind some sixth-graders wearing matching outfits.

"Call me later," Kate says.

"Okay. You're Later. Get the yolk, egghead?"

She rolls her eyes. "Very funny."

I reach the steps, right behind the sixth-grader's flowery backpack. Lovely. Really.

"Seriously," Kate says. "Don't forget to call me. We have to talk strategy."

"About . . . ?"

"Algebra."

There's a tight, peanut-buttery feeling in my throat. What is going to become of me? I suck at math, I suck at soccer.

My legs feel heavy going up the bus stairs. Kate is waving goodbye to me. Making the "call me" hand move with her thumb and pinkie.

I wave, the peanut-butter feeling worse than ever. In minutes she'll find Aaliyah and then her dad will pick up the two of them. He'll take them to their practice over at the lush green fields of Fairfield United and watch intently through the whole thing. Next stop, Swanky Frank's.

That was my life. Now it's not. That was my best friend. It's only a matter of time—days, weeks, if I'm lucky—before Kate gets utterly sucked into the dense black hole of elite soccer.

The bus heads past the soccer fields to the elementary school and we scoop up a bunch of nattering little kids who smell like Elmer's glue and apple juice. Then it's time to drop us all off. I'm the second-to-last stop going home, the second to be picked up in the morning.

When my stop comes, I stand up and glance back. There's

Jasmine, midway down the bus, slouched in her seat next to a little blond girl and staring out the window. The afternoon sun lights one half of her face and leaves the other half in the shadow. Is it just the light or does she look sad? I hesitate, then call, "Bye, Jasmine."

But she doesn't look up.

I can tell that she hears me.

But she doesn't look up.

Jasmine

I sink down in my seat. Please, get off the bus. Because if Maddie keeps thinking about it, she'll put two and two together. She'll figure out I'm one of the Wishbone kids. The stop after hers. She'll find out, and then everyone will find out. And that can't be. I'm new here, equal. No one knows what I've lost, and they're never going to know. I'm not going to face someone else's charity. Someone else's pity. Their feeling that my heart is second-hand, my self marked down. My dad gone, my house, my dog, my life, but I'm still here.

"Jasmine," Breanna whispers. "That girl's yelling for you."

I hold a finger up to my mouth.

"But . . ."

"Shut up," I hiss.

Breanna's eyes get big and shiny. But she stops talking.

Maddie gives up, thank god, and climbs off the bus. We roar away, and I can see her standing there, staring back at me.

When we get off at our stop, Breanna stomps ahead of me. I think of saying sorry, but what's the use? Ian trails behind. Another person to say sorry to.

"Hey, Ian. Sorry. Didn't know about the Hershey's."

"Don't need your apology. Just stay away from us." He turns toward their branch of the Wishbone.

I let myself into our house, shut the door behind me, and lock it. Sit down at the kitchen table, check my phone for messages. There's a text from Mom. *How was your day?* she wants to know. *Great!* I text back. The dots that tell me she's typing. Then: *Don't be a smart aleck.* Me: *Okay. Not great. But not too bad.*

Dots of Mom typing the text: *You know what? This was a big mistake. Awful. Wrong turn for you, me, and Ladybug. Let's go home. Let's go back to Rocky Hill.*

What she does write: *Glad to hear it.*

Suddenly the room spins, and I realize I haven't had anything to eat since that apple in the principal's office this morning. I open the fridge, pull out the carrot cake Mom baked over the weekend, and cut myself a generous slice. Pour a glass of milk and turn on the TV.

The sweetness of the cake, the coldness of the milk. The tangerine of a girl's toenails on TV. Mom's feet hold her up all day long, through two jobs. *Glad to hear it,* Mom had written. Mom needs everything to be okay. If not great, at least not bad.

A knock at the door. My heart springs and hammers.

Harder and harder knocking.

A man's voice asks, "Anybody home?"

Crouch in my chair. Freeze.

Maddie

"Yo, yo, yo, my peeps, you say hello, I say mellow, so bust a move!" Dad shouts when I shuffle into the kitchen, straight off the school bus. Dad does (what he thinks are) hip hop moves around the room. "What's happening?"

"Hey, Dad," I say from inside his hug. "Happening? My math teacher gave us a quiz on the very first day. And we have our first test next Friday." He kisses the top of my head and lets me go.

"Write it right up there in big bold letters." Dad points to the Dry Erase Hall of Fame.

"I can't. I'm starving."

Dad uses his hand as a microphone. "Medic! Get this girl some food." He slides a plate of Monday Snickerdoodles over to me and I take two.

"Thanks, Daddy." Dad and his cookies always put me in a good mood.

Scooter and Pete are busy at their little wooden art table in the corner of the kitchen. "Maddie, I caught a worm," Scooter tells me.

"That's great." I bend down and kiss them both on their bristly blond heads.

"Dad made him put it back," Pete adds.

While I'm sitting at the table eating the cookies and

drinking a glass of cold milk, Lexi comes through the back door, her blond hair flying behind her and a cell phone glued to her ear. She tells me not to be suckered in by all the ads and commercials; blonds don't have more fun. Even if her nose is a little too long for perfect, and there are three tiny moles that make a Bermuda's Triangle on her jaw, it's hard not to believe she's having more fun.

"Gotta go, babe," she says to one of her twenty friends. She listens. "Yep. Cute green T-shirt from Barcelona. It was sweet of Ted."

Once, I practiced saying "Gotta go, babe" in my bedroom mirror, about thirty times. I sounded like a total and absolute dork.

"How was day one?" Dad asks. "Break any hearts or pencils?"

She snatches a cookie off the platter and takes a decisive bite. "Awesome. I got a 105 on our assessment of last year's material."

"How is that even possible?" I say, pushing my chair back and bringing my plate and cup to the dishwasher. "Isn't 100 a perfect score?" Lexi's phone starts buzzing before she can let me into the secrets of Lexi World.

Dad pulls stuff from the fridge—carrots, broccoli, bok choy, ginger. "Help me prep for dinner?" he asks. My favorite chore—chopping—so he doesn't need to ask twice. After washing our hands in the sink and having a mini water-flicking fight, we stand side by side, scraping the thin skin from the carrots, then slicing them into small discs. When we've filled each container, snapped on their lids, and stacked them in the fridge for tonight's stir fry, Dad turns to me, a little frown etched between his eyebrows. "Say, when do you find out about Fairfield United?"

I grab a banana and fiddle with the ugly brown stump, where it was pulled from the plant. Gram told me bananas don't grow on trees. She loved to collect tidbits, as she called them. She loved green bananas, green tomatoes, green tea. Green, she said, was the color of envy, but also of hope. The color of Ireland and Islam. New leaves, jade, emeralds. *Green is your best color, Madeline, because of your lucky green eyes.*

"Maddie? Hellooo?"

"I don't know, Dad. Pretty soon." Dad's eyes rest on me, so I force myself to meet them. Flash a smile. "Fingers crossed."

"Maddie," he begins. But before he can say another word, I head for the stairs and take them two at a time.

Jasmine

Headlights circle around my room like ghosts trying to find their way to heaven. Somebody's leaving the Wishbone: that man who knocked at the door?

Didn't tell Mom about it. No point in adding one more worry to her day.

When he knocked, I stayed as still as cake, drying on a plate. After, I kept the TV off. What if he came back and heard it? Jimmied the lock? Peered through the glass? Instead, I went into my bedroom, closed the curtains, and got on iChat.

I talked to Carly from back home. She pretended Chelsea never happened, so I pretended, too.

Now Mom's home, talking on the phone, softly, so softly, to Uncle Louie and Aunt Gail.

A message from Mikayla pops up on my computer. We chat about our class, Clover, and clothes. She tells me about a boy she likes. She tells me about clothes she wants. There's the sting again. The wish that I only had little things to worry about.

Mom and I don't buy paper towels. We know canned is cheaper than frozen and way cheaper than fresh. I never ask Mom for name-brand stuff. I know we can't afford it. Two hundred bucks for a winter coat? A hundred for a pair of jeans? No way, when you can go to Goodwill and get it for almost nothing.

But when Chelsea's mom took me shopping and bought me everything I tried on—piles of shirts, jeans, leggings. . . . Now I know it's like wearing armor. Clothes from Goodwill can't ever be armor.

"Jas," Mom calls from the kitchen.

I sigh and push off from the green wooden chair that used to be part of someone else's life before we snagged it from Goodwill for seven bucks (along with someone's humongous Christmas ornament collection for ten lousy dollars, and a DKNY leather jacket for Mom for twenty-five—things that Mom first said no to, until I begged her to get them).

"Yeah?" I call from my doorway. Our home is small, but I

like that. Just Mom's bedroom on one side of the hallway and mine on the other. One bathroom off the same hallway, where we share a medicine cabinet and a sink. The kitchen and living room, kind of a combo space.

Mom, floating in a filmy long nightgown, gestures to me to come to the phone. I shake my head. She gestures again, bigger, a scowl carving lines on her face. I trudge to the phone and swipe it from her.

"Hello," I say. Mom sits down at the kitchen table sort of quickly. I wave to get her attention and then I mouth "Sorry, Mom." She smiles—but the smile's a tired one, all in the lips, not in the eyes.

I should have raced to the phone. Shouldn't have given Mom another thing to worry about, and there she is sitting with her bare arms all covered with layers of gold and pink freckles, especially on her shoulders. But her neck, exposed by her ultra-short haircut, is white, protected from the sun by her once-long hair. How Dad loved her hair. He said her hair was butterscotch and mine was dark chocolate. Once I came home and he was brushing it. . . . I wish I hadn't thought it was so weird. Who was I to tell them how to act? If only I could go back to the brat I was in that moment and let Dad brush Mom's hair. Can't.

But I cried harder when she cut it than I did through his whole funeral.

"Hey, there, Princess Jasmine," Uncle Louie booms into the phone. "How you doing?"

"Fine," I say with as much oomph as I can power up, although I wish Uncle Louie wouldn't call me that. Mom's hands are tracing a pattern on the fake-wood table, worrying it. I make myself keep talking. "It's nice," I continue. "You should come over."

"Oh, yeah? They got any Catholic churches in Clover?"

He lives ten minutes away; he knows. Why can't he get into his Dodge pickup and drive here, see his kid sister, see me? Because Uncle Louie doesn't understand why we don't just live in their mother-in-law suite, Mom said. *He doesn't understand that I need to be independent,* Mom told me. I don't understand it, either. "Are you kidding, Uncle Louie? That's all they've got."

"Well, maybe we will," Uncle Louie says. A pause. "You and your mom getting to church yet?"

"Not yet," I say.

"Computer and phone holding up okay?"

"They're both great. Thanks, Uncle Louie."

"Ah, it's nothing. Jasmine, I'm happy things are working out for you and your mom. But you know you've always got a home here just a heartbeat away."

"I know," I say.

Home? That was Dad and Mom and me. But I don't say that.

Because Mom is filling in the blank squares of a puzzle. And that, I haven't seen for a good long time.

Maddie

"Hey, cute stuff," Mom calls from the mudroom. "Yum, smells like stir fry?" She clicks into the kitchen, takes her suit jacket off, and drapes it on the back of a chair, while flipping through the mail. Thank baby Buddha and baby Jesus I decided to load the dishwasher instead of giving in to the temptation to flop on the family room couch and read. Mom holds out her arms and I lean in for a hug, feeling guilty that I don't want to hug her. I love Mom, but we are total opposites, and it bugs her that I can't be more like her: organized, rational, logical. That's what makes Mom so good at what she does, which is to defend magazine publishers from getting sued. Mom spends long hours reading articles on the computer before they're published.

She hugs me tight, leans back and scrutinizes me. "So, how was school?"

Whenever Mom asks me that, she means: *How did you do in school?*

"I don't know. Fine."

"And tryouts? Hear anything?" Mom reaches down to the dishwasher and repositions a plate.

Not again. Dad interrogated me at dinner, right in front of Lexi and the twins. Luckily Scooter threw his broccoli at Pete. Then Pete flung a handful of rice at Scooter. Flying food is a real conversation-stopper.

Dropping dirty knives into the silverware basket, I'm tempted to get it over with and tell her. But I think about the disappointment that she'll try to mask. And the worry. Followed by the flood of advice and suggestions—maybe I should join debate or cross-country or something. She—and even Dad—will miss the point. I don't want to be part of just anything. I want to be part of my old life—with Kate.

Face, stay cool. "Not yet."

Mom grabs a plate and heaps vegetables from the wok and brown rice onto it. She turns to me, two lines creasing her brow. "Don't you usually hear right away?"

"Yeah, but there were so many girls trying out . . ."

"Should I email the coach?" Mom asks through a mouthful of food.

"No," I sigh and drape myself on the kitchen counter. "We'll probably hear tomorrow," I mutter into the granite.

Mom comes closer to me, plate in one hand, and puts her hand on my head. "I'm sure you were great."

"Don't be so sure. Mom, this year it's Fairfield United. Not everybody on travel makes the team."

Her cell phone vibrates loudly on the kitchen table. "We'll talk about this later," she says.

"Okay, Mom. Whatever you say." No, we won't. Because I already said way too much.

Mom talks on her cell phone for a few minutes in a really stern, clipped voice while I finish loading the dishwasher and wiping the counters. Tomorrow's pesto pasta night and it will be Lexi's turn to scrape and load. I loathe scraping pesto. Mom hangs up and scowls at the ceiling. She's totally forgotten about our conversation—and her dinner. Fine with me.

"Are the boys upstairs?" Mom asks.

"Yep, Dad's giving Evil and Satan a bath."

"Madeline Katherine." Mom can't take a joke.

"Sorry." I honestly think every conversation I have with Mom ends with me saying "Sorry."

Shutting the dishwasher, I hurry out of the kitchen, taking the stairs two at a time to my room. Near my sister's door, my sneakers slow and then stop. Sneaking in, I pull open her dresser drawer and dig through her T-shirts. No cute green tee from Barcelona. But there it is, on her desk, next to a pair of denim cut-offs.

"Tell them I'll call back!" Lexi yells from outside her door. "I have to start my Latin homework."

Oh my llama. Snatching the green tee, I jump into her closet, squeezing between clingy plastic dry cleaning bags. Door clicks shut. She launches into "Seasons of Love," from *Rent.* I try not to laugh.

She stops singing and slides open her dresser drawer, stomps to her door and yanks it open. "Maddie," she bellows. "Did you take my shirt?" Then, "Mom? Maddie's not in her room. Is she downstairs? MOM!"

As soon as her feet clatter down the stairs, I get out of her room as fast as I can. Dive for my bed, stuff the green tee under my pillow, and leap up to sit down at my desk. Lexi pokes her head through my door. I jab at my computer to wake it.

"There you are," Lexi says, leaning against my doorjamb, her arms crossed and her face scrunched into a scowl. "Why are you sweating?"

My computer screen glows. A message from Kate pops up.

Kate: *1-800-Math-help.*

Can't talk now, I type, then croak to Lexi, "I'm not sweating."

"I'm looking for my brand-new green T-shirt. It was on my desk and now it's gone."

"Haven't seen it." My voice sounds like I sucked on a helium balloon.

"Really? You wouldn't mind me taking a look in your drawer?" Lexi marches over to my dresser, yanks open the top drawer, digs through it, and then slams it so hard the noise makes me jump. That makes me mad. Why should I have to be nervous in my own bedroom because of my crazy sister who thinks I stole her shirt? Even though I did, why does she automatically assume I did?

"MOM! Lexi's bothering me!"

"Lexi, leave your sister alone!"

Lexi kicks a book out of the way as she stomps out of my room. "If I catch you wearing that T-shirt, I'm going to strangle you."

"With the T-shirt?"

She growls like only I can make her.

Later, my lights are off and I stare at the pencil of moonlight where my curtain doesn't cover my window. I can't sleep. My door opens. Clamp my eyes shut. My bed sinks on one side, and then the other.

"Sweetie," Mom whispers. "Are you awake?"

I keep my eyes still; my lashes flutter, though.

Dad, on the other side. "Maddie," he whispers. "You didn't make the team, did you?"

"No," I whisper. Bricks lift off my chest.

He reaches down and kisses my brow. Mom, for some reason, lifts up my hand and kisses it.

They tiptoe from the room; I fall into a deep inky sleep and dream that I am walking through a grove of birch trees. My black hair is parted down the center and my white dress billows around me. White and black tree, white and black me.

Jasmine

Dream: a black metal bridge and underneath, roaring water. Dad's on the other side, holding out his arms.

"Dad, I'm afraid to fall," I say.

He says, "Falling is the only way to get here."

A WEEK LATER
MONDAY, SEPTEMBER 9

Maddie

I bang out the door just in time to see my school bus pulling away. A blond little girl waves at me.

Dad steps out after me, Sponge Bob coffee cup in hand.

"Did you miss it again?" he asks wearily. "Maddie, you can't keep spacing out and being late every day." His voice notches up a bit in anger. "It doesn't just affect you. It affects all . . ."

We both freeze at the sound of a loud crash, followed by Scooter yelling, "Sorry, Dad!"

"Wait there," Dad barks at me and turns. "Scooter, don't move. I'm coming! If it's broken, don't step on it."

On the drive to school, Scooter is howling in the back seat, Pete whimpering. A muscle jumps in Dad's jaw.

"Dad . . ."

"Don't, Maddie."

"I'm sorry."

"Not good enough. I can't keep picking up your slack."

"It won't happen again, Dad. I swear."

"Don't you think I want to believe that, Maddie?"

"It's true, Dad."

"I hope so, Maddie."

I want to say I'm sorry again, but I won't let myself. And I miss Gram just then. For her, I was "perfectly Maddie." For me, she was pure love. She made me think that getting old could be fun because you stopped caring what people thought of you. *Start now, Maddie. Don't care what people think of you. Because you are perfectly Maddie.*

Jasmine

All the way to school my stomach aches. First, the dream I keep having about Dad lingers on today like campfire smoke. I could see him last night, so close, the way he was before he got sick.

Second, I shouldn't let Maddie bother me. But she does. What is wrong with her, that she can't get on the bus in the mornings? A solid week of school, and she misses the bus almost every day. What would she do if she were me? Just that thought wraps a tight barbed wire around my throat. I lean into the window, grit my teeth against feeling anything else.

Breanna's tugging on my sleeve, pestering me with questions. She wants me to stop at her school and see her classroom. As if I care where her classroom is. Then I'd have to walk the rest of the way to Clover Middle. For some dumb little kid. No thanks.

The school bus pulls up to the elementary school. Little kids stream past us.

"You have to get off," I tell her.

"Please." She grabs my arm. I'm about to shake her off when I notice her hand. It's so small, and her nails, with their pale crescents underneath. . . . I can't explain how that gets me—but it does.

I cover her hand with mine. "Okay."

She scrambles up and we climb off the bus. "Come on," she says. "I told my teacher about you."

I grin down at her. "Oh, you did, did you?" I ask, secretly relieved that Breanna has forgiven me. She pulls me along a hallway that smells like Pine Sol. I think about Mom cleaning the halls of the other elementary school.

Orange and brown paper leaves and a big WELCOME sign decorate the classroom door. Inside, the tiniest lady I have ever seen peers over her desk at me. No wonder she likes teaching kindergarten. She glances up from a stack of papers.

"Mrs. Rohan," Breanna says in an extremely loud voice. "*This* is Jasmine."

The way Breanna announces me, as if I were a celebrity. Good grief.

Mrs. Rohan walks around her desk and looks—up—at me. "So you're Jasmine," she says. She thrusts out her hand. "I'm Mrs. Rohan. Breanna told me you sit with her on the bus. That's a really nice thing." She beams at me. "All right, Jasmine and Breanna, come over here." She grabs an iPad off her desk and ushers us to the SMART Board. We face the camera, Breanna's hair tickling my arm.

"Say 'bees,'" Mrs. Rohan calls.

After she snaps the picture, Mrs. Rohan inspects it. "Perfect," she says. We follow her across the room, where she prints it and tacks it up with a bunch of other pictures. Red construction-paper letters above the corkboard display announce, "Our Families, Ourselves."

My throat tightens with those words. Breanna wraps her arms around my waist. After a second, I hug her back, and it seems like I'm me and somebody else at the same time when I kiss the top of her head.

Soon, other kindergarteners flood into the classroom, and I'm weirdly happy to see a few girls and boys circle around Breanna, yapping like a bunch of puppies.

Mrs. Rohan follows me to the door. I tense up, but all she says is, "Come by and visit anytime."

Float toward the exit, pass a group of fifth-grade boys armpit-farting on their way to class. On another day I would have told them to grow up. But today I laugh.

Maddie

Why am I always walking against hallway traffic? A wall of kids moves toward me on my way to Language Arts. Kate is leaning against her locker, tossing a mini soccer ball up in the air and catching it with one hand.

"Hey, Maddie." She seems genuinely happy to see me.

"How was your weekend?" I say in an awkward, formal way. I know exactly how her weekend was, thanks to calling her parents.

Kate's face falls. "Oh my god, Maddie . . ."

"It's okay."

"It's not okay. I totally forgot to call you after practice . . . and then on Sunday we had to go to my aunt's house."

The last thing I need is for Kate to feel sorry for me. "No worries. I kind of forgot, too . . ."

Her face breaks into a smile. "Oh, you did, too? Whew!"

Aaliyah blows past me in the hallway. Then she wheels around. "Hey, Katie. Come on, girl! We're going to be late for L.A."

Katie?

"Kate," I say. "Do you want to maybe hang out after school . . . I mean, after practice?"

"KA-TIE," Aaliyah yells. "Come on!" As if I were invisible. As if I'm not going to the same class.

"Sure," she says. "After practice." Then she claps her hand to her forehead. "Shoot, I can't. Come on, we're going to be late."

"Gotta get stuff out of my locker," I mumble.

She nods and leaves me behind.

Jasmine

I sprint across the soccer field that separates Clover Elementary from Clover Middle. The buses have already left. I hurry inside, turn the corner to the eighth-grade wing, and *bam,* I slam right into Ian.

He gives me a shove and because I'm already off balance I careen back and fall on my butt. I scramble to my feet. My fist curls, my arm angles back, just like Dad showed me, and I deliver a blow straight to his nose.

"Jesus," he says, turning away. He touches his nose with his fingers. The fuzzy orange halo of Ms. Leoni comes around the corner.

"Jasmine." Ms. Leoni takes a deep breath. "Tell me you didn't just hit Ian."

My arms hang at my side, slack. I'm warm and sick and wish so much I could still be in Breanna's classroom. If I were allowed to go back in time, actually, I'd wind back further, to Dad holding me by my ankles and spinning me around. It was like flying.

"She didn't hit me," Ian says through gritted teeth. "We just ran into each other."

Ms. Leoni looks at him, looks at me. "Really?"

I stare straight at Ms. Leoni. Just because she gave me an apple, she thinks she owns my soul. "Really," I say coolly.

"Come with me, Ian," Ms. Leoni says. "Let's get that nose looked at by the nurse." She grabs him by the arm and marches him away.

Down the hall, Maddie's at her locker, even though she missed the bus. Dad to the rescue.

Maddie

I stare into my open locker. What do I need for L.A.? Poetry journal, *100 Great American Poems.* Jasmine strides up. Her cheeks are flushed and her hair is a mess.

"Are you okay?" I blurt.

"I'm fine."

She doesn't look fine.

"What are you staring at?" she says.

"Nothing."

"Then stop looking at me." Jasmine spins away.

I swallow hard and shuffle into the classroom.

Mr. Carty scrawls *METAPHOR* and *SIMILE* on the SMART Board. "The tools of poetry, metaphors and similes."

Jeremy's hand shoots up. "What's a metaphor and simile?"

"Anybody know?"

This time I raise my hand, and so do a few other people. Mr. Carty calls on Sage, a girl who is in a lot of my classes this year. "A metaphor compares two unlike things," she says. "A simile also compares two unlike things, but it uses 'like' or 'as.'"

"Excellent definition, Sage," Mr. Carty says.

Jeremy's hand shoots up. "I don't get it."

"A metaphor would be when you say, 'I am a stone wall.' A simile would be, 'I am like a stone wall,'" Aaliyah says.

Jeremy's hand shoots up again. He's going to pull a muscle if he keeps this up. Three questions and the day has barely started. "I still don't understand, Mr. Carty."

"If I say I am a stone wall, what am I suggesting?" Mr. Carty asks.

"That you're tough?" Aaliyah calls out.

"Could be," Mr. Carty says.

"You're impenetrable?" I ask.

"Why not?" Mr. Carty flexes his muscles and we laugh.

"You hold things in?" Brendan says.

"Wow. Insightful. Good." Mr. Carty grins. "So that's how metaphors work. By comparing two things that aren't alike on the surface, you begin to see *how* they are alike." Mr. Carty partners us up, boy-girl, boy-girl. He puts me with Brendan and hands us a book with a bookmark sticking out. He tells us to read the poem and figure out the metaphor.

Brendan scoots back and I scoot forward. His knee brushes against mine; I remember our kiss on the Ferris wheel. Does he? Hard to tell.

"Hi," Brendan says. "Everything okay?"

"Yes. Why wouldn't it be?" I try to keep my voice even.

He shrugs. "I don't know. You seemed upset at the beginning of class."

I rattle the book at him. "Let's figure this out."

We read the poem together. It's called "Fog," by Carl Sandburg:

The fog comes
on little cat feet.

It sits looking
over harbor and city
on silent haunches
and then moves on.

Brendan raises one eyebrow at me, and with it, the little hockey-stick scar. "What do you think?"

"Easy," I say. "He's comparing the fog to a cat."

"Easy for you," he says with a grin.

I stare at the white fleck on his front tooth. It's like a tiny wing.

"What about the part where it's looking?" Brendan says, jabbing at the words with his finger. "How can fog look at something?"

I punch Brendan lightly on the arm, but he grabs it and groans.

"You can't be so literal-minded," I tell him.

Mr. Carty glances up, glances down. I swear he has supersonic hearing.

"Well," I say, thinking. "It can't really. But he makes you think of how fog appears and disappears mysteriously—the way a cat does. So he convinces you that fog can really look at a city, the way a cat might."

"Oh," Brendan says, shrugging. "Why didn't he say so?"

I clap a hand over my mouth to smother a giggle.

We write up our analysis quickly. I start to doodle all over the page, just barely stopping myself from making a fancy "B."

"How was your weekend?" he asks.

I shrug. "Okay, I guess."

"You don't sound too sure."

"Kind of boring." I don't tell him how every time I called Kate, one of her parents answered the phone and told me exactly where she was. As if I was supposed to feel better that she was at Aaliyah's house Friday after school or that the two of them were at some team bonding event on Saturday night. Dad: "I thought you said you were hanging with Kate tonight?" And Mom, deftly making matters worse: "Do you want me to call the Millers for you?"

"Are you playing rec soccer?"

I shake my head. "Nah. It wouldn't be fun without Kate."

"You don't love soccer, right?"

"Nope. But my mom thinks I need to play a sport because my big sister does. Now they're promoting basketball." I think, though, about how they let me tell them the truth in the dark of my bedroom and how they didn't mention soccer again. How Lexi gave me a rib-cracking hug the next morning. She knew I got cut and said nothing.

"I wonder why they do that. Force you to do stuff."

"Do yours?"

He hesitates for a moment, bites his thumb. "Naw, they let me do pretty much what I want."

"That's cool."

"I think it's because they feel guilty."

"Guilty?"

He feels the scar on his eyebrow and strokes it. "You know. Because of the divorce."

I nod sympathetically. "How are the guidance meetings? Do they help?"

He clenches his jaw, cracks his knuckles. "That's the worst part. Talking about my feelings. If I wanted to talk about it, it wouldn't be to some counselor who eats pistachios while I'm talking."

My eyes widen. "He does not."

"She. And yes, she does."

"Sensitive."

He rolls his eyes. "Tell me about it." But he smiles. It reminds me of the time I melted frozen butter in the microwave. It went from frozen to explosion in ninety seconds. And so do I.

Eventually Mr. Carty catches on that the majority of the class has finished analyzing the poems. He requests that we share by reading the poems aloud and offering our analysis. Brendan lets me do the talking. Then Mr. Carty zings us with in-class writing.

"Get out your notebooks," he says. "Time to write your own poems with your own fabulous metaphors. Here's the thing: I want every line to begin with 'I am.' Go back to the Sylvia Plath poem 'Metaphors' for inspiration."

We groan.

"At least five lines."

Deafening roar of protest. Then we write.

Jasmine

Sarah, Mikayla, and I sit in the grass on the sidelines, waiting for the gym teacher to make an appearance. Ian studies me from the soccer field. He lets me know it, too. Jesus, how long can you hold a grudge? I waited for him to come down the hallway after the nurse. I apologized, said it was a gut reaction and really stupid and he could hit me back if he wanted. What more does he want?

Mikayla says, "What's his problem?"

"It's a long story." I keep myself busy plucking grass.

Mikayla shrugs. "He probably likes you."

I laugh like a crow's caw. "I doubt it."

"He's kind of cute," Sarah says. "If gingers are your type."

"I'm all good with that," Mikayla says. "But somebody needs to help him with his personal style. Like, I don't really need to see that much of his socks."

"Maybe his parents can't afford new pants," I say. It doesn't come out as lightly as I want.

"That's for sure," Sarah says and her voice drops. "He lives in that trailer court by Stop & Shop. One time in sixth grade my mom picked him up walking down Post Road in the pouring rain. It was sad. And embarrassing."

My finger burrows past the blades of grass to find the dirt. I dig at it with my fingernail. Only so much you can bury in the dirt. What if I told my new "friends" that I live on the Wishbone, too? What would they think of me then?

"You know, this is probably wrong of me to say, but I really don't get how people can just raise their kids that way," Mikayla says. She leans back in the grass and cups her hand over her eyes. "Like, if you can't afford to have kids, don't have them."

An expression settles on my face and I know—I just know it—I look like Dad. Proud, angry, but holding it all in. Chin thrust out, teeth biting down.

"Don't look now," Sarah says under her breath. "The poet who didn't know it."

Maddie comes jogging up. She stands in front of us, twisting one long strand of hair around her index finger. "Hey, guys," she says.

"Hey, Maddie," I say. I'm the only one who speaks. But Maddie seems oblivious that they dissed her. It occurs to me that her innocence—and her total lack of awareness that they are the queen bees—is exactly what makes Sarah and Mikayla so mad.

"We just found out outdoor gym was cancelled. Mr. Gulden tripped and sprained his ankle," Maddie tells us.

"Oh, thank you, Jesus," Sarah says. She hops up and extends her hand down to me. Maddie glances at me uncertainly and says something under her breath, then shuffles away.

"Oh, wow," Mikayla says. "You've got a fan, Jasmine."

"Not a fan," I say lightly. "A friend."

"Um, no," Sarah says.

"No?"

"She's in la-la land. She's Library Girl."

Mikayla wraps her arms around herself. "Although . . ."

Sarah narrows her eyes. "What?"

"Brendan Cohen likes her."

"Then maybe's he's not as hot as he used to be. Seriously. Would you look at what she's wearing today?"

"I'm bored," I announce, just to shut them up. "Can we talk about something else?"

Lift the heavy weight of my hair off my neck, but the sticky air offers no relief. Think that maybe if I gave Maddie some tips on how to dress, her life would be a tad bit easier. My good deed for this girl who seems to need one.

Put your best face to the world, Dad said. Maddie seems to only have this one face—innocent smile, hopeful green eyes. She has had things easy all her life, that I'm sure of.

Maddie

We're down to four people at our lunch table: me, Kate, Megan, and Emma. Jasmine deserted after just one day—lured by the star power of Sarah and Mikayla. Rachel and Sorcha were the surprise defections. They tried out for—and made—the volleyball team. Now that's where they sit—with the volleyball kids. My hands pick up a taco, but my stomach doesn't want to eat it. Wish I could just get a cookie today. Wish Mom and Dad would let me buy from the a la carte line. Kate must know she belongs to the soccer-girls table, where we all crowded together last year. But she's holding back for me. I want her to go, but I want her to stay with me even more.

"Can I sit with you guys?" Aaliyah sits down before anyone can answer.

They plunge straight into soccer talk, and my brain reaches a planet not detected by NASA. Megan, toward the end of lunch, suddenly scrapes back her chair and walks off without a word.

"What's her problem?" Kate says.

"I think she asked you the same question three times in a row," Aaliyah says to me.

"No, she didn't," I say, thinking: *Did she?*

After lunch, Ms. Bonner hands back our tests from Friday. I got a D. She asks me if I can stay after school for extra help and I say yes, but when I stop by her classroom at the end of the day, she's busy talking to someone else. I sneak back out of the room.

In line for Bus One, I glance over my shoulder, worried that Ms. Bonner will come out and yell at me. Which she obviously won't. It's not kindergarten. She doesn't care if I pass her class or fail it. But still.

Jasmine taps me on my shoulder and I jump. She laughs. "Sorry to scare you. And sorry Sarah and Mikayla aren't very friendly."

I shrug. "They're friendly enough to you." To change the subject, I point to her boot. "Your lace is untied."

"Thanks." She smiles her breathtaking smile, then leans down to lace up her boot.

"Where did you get them?" I itch one foot with the other.

Jasmine looks at her boot, the smile erased from her face. "I don't remember."

I swallow hard and glance around. Brendan's on his bus line, talking to Jeremy, and off in the distance Sarah and Mikayla are on the car pick-up line. Why is it so hard to talk to Jasmine? Everything I say annoys her.

"My sister would love them." I just can't seem to stop talking, though.

Jasmine's expression is cold. She looks away. Then looks back. "You don't care that much about clothes, though, do you?"

I think my clothes are nice. They came from a store that my Mom has shopped at since I was a little kid. "No, I guess not," I say.

I slouch onto the bus.

At home, I walk straight through the kitchen and up to my room, throw myself on the bed, and burst into tears.

Someone knocks at the door. "Go away," I sob.

The door opens. "I can't," Dad says. "My little girl is crying. It's in the Parent Handbook that you can't go away when your little girl is crying. How about some Snickerdoodles?"

"I don't want any. And I'm not little, Daddy," I sob. "I'm old."

Dad sits on the edge of my bed. "If you're old, I must be . . ." He deepens his voice and says dramatically. "The Crypt Keeper!"

"That's not funny, Dad." But I smile a little bit. And Dad has an ink smudge on his nose. Whenever he has a new client, he gets so caught up, he's always all inky.

"What's up, buttercup? Spill the beans. 'Fess up. What happened? Did you get hit in the head with a tetherball?"

"No." I smile even more. Dad is funny. If it were Mom, she would tell me to get a grip.

"Did you get sent back to sixth grade? Did you sit next to somebody who had a gas problem?"

With each question, I shake my head and laugh. "Okay, I'll tell you." I pause. "I realized that my clothes are really stupid."

Dad snaps his head back like a turtle. "Seriously? You gave them an IQ test?"

"Dad! I'm a dork."

He frowns. "No. I don't like you saying that about yourself."

"Okay, I dress like a dork. I need new clothes."

"Really? Kate, too?"

"Well, not Kate. But she's a jock."

"Maddie, honey," Dad says in a more serious voice. "You know I made art before I became a graphic designer?"

"Yeah?" I'm trying to follow my way through the maze. Enter at dork, end at Dad as artist.

"Sometimes people who care passionately about art or music or words . . . don't care so much about clothes.

They're so focused on this one thing that everything else fades away. It was that way for me. Is it that way for you sometimes?"

I breathe in, huff it out. "You mean I'm a dork?"

"I mean maybe you care about books and life and friendships . . . and less about appearances?"

"No. I care about appearances." I have no idea why, but my eyes are filling with tears.

"Okay," Dad says carefully, as if the room might explode if he talks too loud. "Since when?"

"Dad. Since today. And how do you know, Dad? You're a guy. Girls are different. And Mom is never around to ask about this stuff." I look up at him. He sighs and looks out my window.

"Listen, Maddie, I hear what you're saying. But you have to make a contribution, too. These brand-name clothes are very expensive."

I nod. Even though we have a nice house and go on nice vacations, Mom and Dad don't like to waste money. They're big into sales.

"How about I pay for half? I saved money from babysitting for Aunt Tina this summer."

"Fine," Dad says. "If this is how you want to spend it."

Dad texts Lexi and we head to the mall with the twins in tow. The twins have a blast, eating kettle corn and zooming around the potted plants. The four of us zip into the stores that I've always known about, but never went into. They seemed too dark and stinky and loud for me. And they're still too loud for the twins, who keep their fingers in their ears. Dad has to hold Pete at Abercrombie because he's afraid of the giant moose head on the wall.

At home, I lug my shopping bags up the front walk.

Lexi's on the porch, on her cell. "Ted, I told you, I already said yes to Eric," she says into the phone. "Sorry, dude."

Gasp. She's got the green T-shirt I wore last week bunched up in her hand. I try to walk past her but she says, "Gotta go," and grabs me by the arm. "You stunk up my shirt. And you drew on it. I found it in the back of my closet. Like you thought you could get away with wearing it."

"I did not!" I yelp.

"Stop lying, Maddie. Dad, you have to tell her to stop borrowing my stuff without asking. It's not fair!"

"Okay, Maddie, take that shirt and wash it, dry it, and return it to your sister, now," Dad says in a stern tone I hardly ever hear. None of us do.

"No, she'll ruin it, Dad," says Lexi. "It's got to be hand-washed and line-dried."

"But Dad, I borrowed it because I didn't have anything to wear."

"You heard your sister. Hand-wash, line-dry." Dad points to my shopping bags. "Or how about Lexi borrows one of your new things?"

"Fine!" I snatch the green T-shirt from Lexi and storm

through the kitchen door and up to the laundry room.

"And you have Lexi's chores for one week," Dad calls after me.

After I've hand-washed the organic green T-shirt, I hang it up on the indoor clothes line and I head to my bedroom. I know Lexi had a right to be mad that I wore her shirt. But did she have to be such a jerk about it? I grab my notebook and flop on my bed and write:

I am a knife, slicing through hard bread.
I am an ax, chopping down a tree.
I am scissors cutting thick hair.
I am the hook, the line, and the sinker.
I am lightning, cracking open the sky.
I am a pin, piercing a butterfly.

TUESDAY, SEPTEMBER 10

JASMINE

A ray of sunlight slides through the gap where my old curtain doesn't cover my new window. I open my eyes, glance at my alarm clock, realize I forgot to set it. If I don't hurry, I'm going to miss the bus like Maddie.

Groaning, I roll out of bed. The last thing I want to do is go to school, but I know I have to. I pad into the kitchen and see the note that Mom left me on the table.

Jazzy,

There's carrot sticks and some leftover lasagna in the fridge in case you are hungry after school.

Be a good girl.

Mom

I pour myself a bowl of store-brand cereal and drizzle a little milk on it. There's nothing I hate more than soggy cornflakes. I also hate the sound of silence, but today I have to hurry.

In the quiet of the house, I brush my teeth, wash my face, and brush my hair. The whole while, I have the strange feeling that someone is watching me. I let myself out of the house, locking the door. The muggy Connecticut air captures me in a hug.

A hand clamps onto my shoulder.

I jump straight into the air and let out a yelp, like a dog who got its tail caught in the door.

"Hey, hey!" The man with the orange crew cut raises his hands like I just stuck him up with a gun. "It's only me, your neighbor. I'm Mr. Albert, from the other side of the court."

I recognize the voice—the man who knocked on our door the first day of school. I take a step backward. Turn my nose away from his breath, which smells sour, like cigarettes and beer. He holds up a jar of Smucker's jam, then thrusts it in my hands.

"Welcome to the neighborhood," he says. "Your mom said she likes peanut butter and jelly sandwiches." Up close, I see that he has a small deep scar by the corner of his right eye. Make a note of it in case he's wanted by the police. "I met her the other day," he says. His words run together. "Maybe you and she could come over and have dinner?"

"No, we can't." A few other kids who live on the other side of the trailer court round the corner and trudge through the mucky air toward the bus stop. After a deep breath, I say, "Excuse me," setting the jam down on the porch railing and pushing past him. He catches my wrist.

"Can I just say hi to your mom?"

I wrench my wrist free. "She's not home right now," I say, then instantly regret my words, floating out in the air like black flies. "She just went to the store."

"Ah-ha," he says, holding up one finger and swaying a little bit.

What does he mean by *ah-ha*?

I push past him. "I have to go," I say.

"*Parting is such sweet sorrow*," he calls after me. "That's Shakespeare!" he adds as I race over to the bus stop, crossing the patch of yard dotted with little white-flowered weeds and bigger weeds like cabbages. The muggy air makes me feel like I'm tumbling inside the dryer with a load of towels. Somewhere in the distance, bells ring. There are so many churches in this town. Every hour, every half hour, the bells ring. It's annoying. Who needs to know that much about the time?

"What did my dad want?" Breanna asks me. She points over my shoulder.

I exhale, piece it together. Breanna Albert. "Your dad? Nothing."

Ian comes racing around the corner. "Wait for me!" he hollers as the bus pulls up.

"He got late 'cause he had to clean up the mess."

Thinking of the beery smell on Mr. Albert's breath, I open my mouth to ask what kind of mess. Then I think better of it. *Mind your own business*, Ian had said. Maybe I will.

Maddie

Last night, when they thought we were all asleep, Mom and Dad went at it.

"She has you wrapped around her little finger!" Mom yelled at Dad.

"She's going through a tough time."

"Tough time? She's thirteen. She doesn't even know what tough is. Tough is paying the mortgage. Tough is having a client who doesn't understand that you're not in their time zone."

I wrapped myself around in my sheet, around and around until I couldn't breathe, and pressed my ear into my pillow. But it didn't block the sound of a slammed door.

This morning Mom's long gone, on the 6:46 to Grand Central.

Now, over our bowls of cornflakes, Lexi's giving me a funny look as she takes in my Abercrombie sweatshirt. "You look like a billboard."

"What do you mean?"

"Maddie, don't you realize you're a tool for the company, advertising their products?"

"All right, Comrade," Dad says from the counter where he's packing up the twins' lunches. "You've made your point."

"I don't understand what you're talking about." My voice shakes, I'm so angry. "You've always been able to be whoever you want to be, say whatever you want to say, wear whatever you want to wear."

Lexi stops. Dad stops. Pete looks up from his crayon drawing of a rectangle on wheels.

"I've never criticized you. I never told you not to care about whales or literacy or world hunger. I never told you not to wear your hair long or not to be friends with someone. So why is it okay for you to do that to me?" I stop, not because I don't have more angry words, but because I'm out of breath.

"Sorry," Lexi says quietly.

And she grabs her backpack and heads out the door without another word.

If I'm right, why do I feel so bad?

At school, Kate stares at me, taking in the whole outfit. "What happened here? It looks like you collided with Sarah and Mikayla."

"I got some new clothes." I cram a notebook into my locker. It falls out.

"Yeah, but . . . didn't you and your mom already go back-to-school shopping?"

I shove the notebook back in and then slam my locker shut.

"Is this to impress that new girl?"

"No." How can I explain to Kate everything I'm scared about? She's got soccer and a whole team of friends.

"You're a ridiculous liar, Maddie." She slams her locker and heads into Language Arts.

I follow her, my feet already sweaty inside these sheepskin boots.

Mr. Carty is in fine form. "Today, my friends, we're going

to partner up and learn a little bit about poetic forms."

Chorus of groans. I cheer inside and cross my fingers, hope to die, that I get to be partners with Brendan. But when Mr. Carty assigns partners, I get Jasmine.

"We've got villanelle," I say unnecessarily. She has the same piece of paper in front of her. She stares at the page, hunched over.

I read the definition to myself. A villanelle is a French form of poetry. Five stanzas × three lines = fifteen lines + one stanza of four lines = nineteen lines altogether.

I turn to the next page in the packet. I remember Gram reading this poem aloud—"Do Not Go Gentle Into That Good Night." It was about not giving in to death easily. I close my eyes for a second, remembering Gram's voice, rough from years of smoking cigarettes. She quit, but too late.

"My grandma loved this poem." I hold my breath, hoping that I won't say the wrong thing again.

Jasmine looks up at me with her steady, serious eyes. Quietly, so quietly, she speaks. I lean forward, press my ribs into the edge of my desk, to hear her.

"What's the point of fighting against death?" she says. "You're not going to win. Nobody does."

Jasmine

Buttery popcorn smell in the air; *clack-clack* of the fan overhead; Mom's narrow feet in my lap. I consider my Scrabble letters, then make my move.

"Um, I'm pretty sure 'EX' is not a word," Mom says. Her eyes crease even before she smiles.

"Is that a challenge I hear?"

"No, smarty-pants." Mom takes a big drink of her Pepsi. "I'll let you have it. But how 'EX' got you thirty-one points is beyond me. So, homework . . . ?"

"All done, as I already told you."

"I know. Just want to be sure. What's your favorite class?"

"Hmm. Algebra. Yes, definitely."

Mom studies the words. Her eyes widen, then she gathers up her tiles. "G-E-O-G-R-A-P-H."

"'Geograph'? Mom, *A*, that's not a word, and *B*, how can you still have a tile left? You're only supposed to have seven tiles."

Mom looks so disappointed I almost want to let her have the points. Then she brightens up again. She lifts "GEO" from the board and leaves "GRAPH."

I record her fourteen points and contemplate my options. It leaps out at me: "CRAZY." I could spell it and get sixty-nine points.

"How about English?" Mom asks. "How do you like that?"

"It's fine," I say.

Mom lifts my chin, her fingers icy from her Pepsi. "Kids are nice?"

"Mom," I force myself to laugh. "They're fine. They're great, okay?"

"Maybe you should invite someone over this weekend. You know, to hang out?"

And then I think of Maddie. Ian told me to mind my own business. I told Maddie to mind hers. But maybe neither of us can help caring about somebody else's business.

Should I invite Maddie over to the Wishbone?

Or would she feel like Sarah and Mikayla? Wonder why poor people have kids? Would she be like Chelsea, and give me her hand-me-downs? Or would it be something worse? Some weird torture I haven't even thought of yet. Like she'd start writing poems about the poor girl whose dad died and who had to go live at the Wishbone.

"Okay, Mom, I'll invite a friend over if you make haystacks."

"Deal."

I lay down my tiles. "DOG."

Mom raises an eyebrow. "Really? That's the best you can do?"

"Yep," I say, my second lie of the night.

But the thought lingers. Can I trust Maddie with the truth about myself?

Someone knocks on the door. Mom half-stands. Another knock.

"Hello?" It's friggin' Mr. Albert.

"What do you want?" I yell out.

"Hey, Jasmine," Ian calls back. Even through the door I can tell he's embarrassed.

Mom smiles. "Oh, it's just Pete. He's harmless." Her voice drops. "Drinks too much."

I unlock the door and there is Mr. Albert, holding a pan of brownies—with potholders on his hands. The brownies smell good. Ian stands next to him, his hands thrust into his pockets.

"Are those for us?" Mom asks in a way-too-friendly voice. "That's nice of you."

"Dad wanted to welcome you guys to the neighborhood. Again," Ian explains.

Our eyes meet.

I say, "Thanks, Mr. Albert."

Mr. Albert looks over my shoulder. "Ah, Scrabble. Have either of you added 'IZENED' to 'DEN' to make 'DENIZENED'?"

"Nope," I say.

"It can be worth 212 points."

"No way." I'm drawn in despite myself.

Ian takes his hand out of his pocket, points his thumb at his dad. "He used to be an English teacher. He's a Scrabble whiz."

Mr. Albert beams. "Well, not a whiz, exactly."

"Wait . . . who's watching Bre?" I ask.

"She's asleep," Ian admits. "We've gotta go back."

"What if she wakes up?" I say, taking one step toward the door. "She'd be scared."

"She sleeps like a log," Ian says. "And snores."

I can't help but grin.

Mr. Albert sways a little on his feet. Mom, her own hands now potholdered, takes the pan from him. "This was very kind of you," she says. She looks pointedly at me.

"Thank you," I say. Then, stupidly, I say to Ian, "Maybe you guys could come over and play Scrabble some time."

"I suck at it," Ian says.

"'The moment of change is the only poem,'" Mr. Albert says to Ian. "Adrienne Rich's words, not mine."

"'You can make it if you try,'" Mom adds. "Mick Jagger's words, not mine."

Ian and I simultaneously roll our eyes.

And we leave it at that.

WEDNESDAY, SEPTEMBER 11

Maddie

Mr. Carty tortures us a little more. Each "partnership" will be assigned one Great American Poet.

"GAP, for short," Mr. Carty says. "You will become a literary expert on that poet. You will read a substantial body of work. And you will learn all the major biographical facts about that poet."

Jeremy's hand not only goes up, it waves around like a wind-whipped flag. Mr. Carty ignores him.

"Together you will present both a written report and a PowerPoint about your poet," Mr. Carty says, and Jeremy's hand sinks. "Pick a poet partner."

Sarah and Mikayla grab each other like they're on lifeboats. Kids jump up, call out names. Aaliyah moves toward Kate, but before she can reach Kate's desk, Dani grabs Aaliyah's arm. They pair up and Kate keeps reading her book.

Just when I'm about to jump up and head to Kate, Brendan turns around in his chair. He opens his mouth to speak, and I open my mouth, too. Before either of us can say anything, Jasmine is standing by my desk.

"Partners?" she says to me.

"Okay," I say, stunned into agreement. Brendan shrugs and turns away. Darn, darn, darn. I can't believe I agreed.

I'm warm all of a sudden inside my new sweatshirt, so I yank it off and drape it over the back of my chair.

All the kids pair up.

But one kid's left over. Kate. Now that we're about to head to the library, I can't help but look at her. She's deep into reading a David Beckham biography.

"Silly me," Mr. Carty says. "With everyone here today, we have twenty-three students. An odd number."

"Mr. Carty," I say. "Kate, Jasmine, and I can be partners. Come on, Kate."

Kate glances up from her book and Jasmine studies a poster on the wall like it started talking. Mr. Carty hands us each the name of our GAP to research. I unfold ours and read: *Emily Dickinson.* Oh, lucky day. The wild-nights poet. We already know a bit about her from Mr. Carty.

Jeremy raises his hand. "Do I have to have Walt Whitman?"

"Yep."

Brendan shows me his. "Gwendolyn Brooks." He raises an eyebrow, and I give a thumbs-up.

Sarah chortles, "Yes! We got e. e. cummings. So easy."

"Maybe not as easy as you think," Mr. Carty says.

Walking to the library, Jasmine doesn't say a word.

"Thanks for letting me glom on with you guys," Kate says.

"Natch," I say. "Speaking of math," I add. Kate and I laugh—one of our old jokes, ever since her sister once said, "Speaking of brown dogs," at dinner when no one was talking about brown dogs at all. "I cannot believe Ms. Bonner announced another test in two weeks."

"Sucks," Kate agrees. "Wanna come over after school and study for it?"

"You mean after practice?"

"Der."

"Then, *der*. Yes."

"You can come, too," Kate offers to Jasmine.

Jasmine shakes her head. "I already have plans." *Brr*. If words were water, four ice cubes would've clinked.

In the library, Mrs. Eilertsen gives us a SMART Board presentation on how to research our poet. As soon as we get started on the computer, Kate has to go to the bathroom. Mrs. Eilertsen rolls her eyes but gives her a hall pass.

"Be right back," she says and jogs out of the room.

"Kate, walk," Mrs. Eilertsen calls after her. Getting Kate to walk is like getting a puppy to read the newspaper.

"Okay. Now that Krater is gone, why'd you do that?" Jasmine says.

"Why did I do what?"

"Have her join us. I thought we could do this together."

"What did Kate ever do to you?" I ask.

She shrugs. "She didn't even look at me on the first day of school. And she's pretty much ignored me ever since."

I smile, relieved. "Don't take it personally. When she's reading about soccer, the world doesn't exist. She's just started that David Beckham biography. You saw how she was when it was time to pick partners."

"She's obsessed. Her hair is a disaster. She dresses like a boy."

I push my chair back to get a better look at Jasmine. "What are you getting so nasty for?"

Jasmine's face folds in on itself, like origami. After that, she gets up to find a book. She returns and writes down facts. But she doesn't talk to me.

When Kate comes back, Jasmine's hand shoots up. "Can I please use the bathroom?" she asks Mrs. Eilertsen, her voice cracking on the last word.

Kate glances at me. I shrug. Jasmine jumps up, snatches the hall pass from Mrs. Eilertsen's hand, and runs out the door.

Mrs. Eilertsen's mouth drops open. She stares after Jasmine and turns to me. "What happened?"

"I don't know," I answer. All I can think of is the cliché "a mountain out of a mole hill." Jasmine was hurt by Kate ignoring her, but the hurt seems as big as a mountain. Why?

Jasmine

Stumble out of the library, fists clenched, eyes stinging. I don't belong.

I stand there, in front of the "Books, The Other Channel" poster. Stare down at the floor that's made up of squares, the squares making a hallway, the hallway that's supposed to connect things up. But I feel so lost. A Goodwill toy missing parts. Maddie and Kate fit together. Sarah and Mikayla, too. No matter what I do to wedge in, I don't fit. They have families. They know how their whole life is going to turn out.

Mom and me, without Dad. How's that supposed to work?

A teacher walks by and shoots me a look, so I make my feet move forward. Pass by another teacher, leading a special-needs boy down the hall, a bandana around his neck.

And I know other kids have it worse. Maybe that boy. Maybe kids with no parents at all or parents who hate them, parents who beat them, hurt them. Wrong or right, I only know what I've lost. Dad showing me how to cast a line. Dad who made peanut-butter-chocolate-chip pancakes on Sunday mornings. Dad thinking about community college. Dad telling me bedtime stories about a girl named Super Jazz, stories with ridiculous twists and turns that somehow ended just right. No one, not even Mom, will ever tell me those stories again.

I never went to Dad's grave, and Mom said that was okay. I couldn't bear to think of him in the ground.

My feet move past the lockers, past water fountains.

Back to Carty's classroom.

It's empty. Carty must be in the faculty lounge. My feet carry me to Maddie's desk. Stupid girl with her stupid sweatshirt. Still has the tags on it. If I brought it back to the store, could I get money for it? Money for a bus ticket? Money to go home to Rocky Hill? See Dad's grave. Say goodbye.

I snatch it, stride from the room, my boots crunching a mechanical pencil dropped on the floor. Safe in the hallway, I open my locker, stuff the sweatshirt deep into my backpack, then slam the door shut.

"Jasmine." A hand on my shoulder. I whirl around.

Ms. Leoni's cloud of orange hair is even wilder today. "Everything okay?" she asks in the quietest of voices.

"F-fine," I stammer.

"Where's your class?"

"Library. I had to get something from my locker."

She nods.

I turn and walk back quickly to the library. This time my brain is in charge, not my feet.

It's not until I reach the library that I realize I have nothing in my hands. Nothing that I got from my locker. Ms. Leoni's too smart not to notice.

So why didn't she say anything?

Maddie

As soon as Jasmine leaves, Kate and I jot down Emily facts. My stomach churns. What triggered Jasmine's Kate-hate?

Mrs. Eilertsen sidles up to us. "Oh, Emily Dickinson is your poet. How wonderful." She quotes:

Hope is the thing with feathers
that perches in the soul

and sings the tunes without the words
and never stops at all.

Of course, Brendan walks by right then and gives me the raised eyebrow.

After Jasmine returns, we check out our books, and I pray that Mrs. Eilertsen won't break into verse again. Thankfully, she doesn't.

As we wait for the rest of the class to finish, Jasmine wanders over to Sarah and Mikayla. I crack open *The Poetry of Emily Dickinson*. Kate leans on me and says, "All this poetry has worn me out." My eye catches on:

I'm nobody! Who are you?
Are you nobody, too?
Then there's a pair of us—don't tell!
They'd banish us, you know.

"This poem is kind of cool." I read the first stanza to her.

"AABC rhyme scheme," Kate says.

I elbow her and read on:

How dreary to be somebody!
How public, like a frog
To tell your name the livelong day
To an admiring bog!

Kate frowns.

Me, too. "Oh. She actually likes being a nobody." I want to be a frog. A public frog with a bogful of friends. Like Jasmine, who leans, one boot against the wall, book-ended by Mikayla and Sarah. Her smile's broad and bright, eclipsing all of us.

Settled into Algebra under the air-conditioning vent, I rub my goose-pimpled arms. Reach into my backpack for my sweatshirt and come up empty.

Ms. Bonner gives me a pass to look for it. After checking my locker, I go to the lost-and-found in a corner of the cafeteria. I dig through all the old ketchup-and-mustard-stained jackets and musty, pilled sweaters, and can't find it anywhere. Then I remember: I left it in Mr. Carty's classroom. But Mr. Carty, who is grading papers at his desk, hasn't seen it.

"It'll rutabaga," he says.

I smile feebly. "'It'll turn up' is a cliché?"

"You know it."

By the end of the day, it hasn't. What am I going to tell Dad? I hope he won't notice. Lately it seems like he notices everything.

Every bad thing I do.

Jasmine

Mom comes home while I'm sitting at the table, eating a bowl of heated-up spaghetti. "Hey, Jazzy," she says and kisses me on my head. She smells like the cleaner she uses to wipe the cafeteria tables, her last task as a custodian. "How was today?" she asks, her voice husky—with tenderness or tiredness, I can't be sure.

"Great," I say, searching for the right tone to give my words truth. Because Mom can ferret out a lie. But she gives a quick nod, heads to Dad's La-Z-Boy easy chair. I remember sitting in that chair with him, my ear pressed against his chest, while he held a mystery above my head and read.

I follow her, curl up in her lap; she strokes my long hair off my forehead. "This is the hair I ordered." She sighs.

"Your choice," I remind her, looking up at her cropped hair.

"Still on that topic?"

"Yep."

She glances at the clock and wrinkles her nose. I follow her look. One hour and fifteen minutes before she leaves for her second job at Jungle Fashion. We stay there for a moment, just rocking, between one thing and another. I wish I could stay here forever.

I sit up in her lap. "Let me go with you."

She shakes her head. "Remember how that worked out last time? You didn't write the poem."

"Please, Mom." I squeeze her arm. "I promise. Besides, I already have most of my homework done. Just have to work a little on our Emily Dickinson report." I lean back and nuzzle her neck. "Please."

She laughs. "Stop tickling me."

I nuzzle her some more. "Please."

"Okay. But bring your homework. And do it." She leans back to get a good look at me, then shakes her finger. "No more wandering around the mall."

Mom turns Ladybug into the parking garage expertly and drives up the ramp. I sit next to her, my backpack between my feet, the Abercrombie sweatshirt rolled tight underneath my homework binder.

At first we were both afraid of parking garages. They don't have any in Rocky Hill. The ceilings hang down low, held up by fat concrete pillars. It's dark, too. But it was either park in the parking garage or take the bus to work. Mom got used to it. It was just one of those things Mom had to figure out, like navigating highways clogged with trucks and cars unwilling to let a Toyota Tercel merge or change lanes.

We enter the mall through the Target and stop at the dollar rack to see if there's anything worth buying. I want to buy rawhide for the dog I've seen around the Wishbone, but Mom says we're not about to start feeding animals.

"Please, Mom?" I say, tucking my arm in hers. "It's only a buck."

She frowns—then flashes a smile. "Okay, fine," she says. "But hurry it up."

We stand behind a tattooed woman buying a cartload of Tide and pay for the rawhide. Heading out into the mall, we stride quickly past couples—her pants low, his pants even lower—past Claire's, Gap, and Abercrombie & Fitch, toward Jungle Fashion, where Mom works Monday through Saturday from five to nine. Jungle Fashion is kind of tacky, Mom says, but the people are nice and it pays well, for retail.

Mom and I say hi to Tannis, her coworker, who is probably twenty-two—ten years younger than Mom.

"Hey, gorgeous," Tannis says to me. We fist-bump, our little joke, as if we were on a sports team. She looks me up and down, then sighs. "You look so much better than I ever did in those jeans."

"Don't give her a big head," Mom scolds. "She already knows she's beautiful."

"No, I don't," I say, following Mom to the back, where she clocks in and drops her purse. "Okay if I get a pretzel at the food court?" I ask Mom quickly, when she's busy.

She hands me five dollars. She never says no to food. She focuses on me as I turn to walk out. "You don't need your backpack, sweetie. Leave it here. And don't talk to anyone."

I nod, cursing under my breath.

Tannis asks Mom a question about markdowns on some leftover tank tops, and Mom turns to answer her. I dart away, backpack intact.

I make a beeline for Abercrombie & Fitch. It stinks like men's deodorant. Dad wouldn't be able to stand it. The darkness and the throbbing music make me dizzy. I head straight to the register, pull the sweatshirt out of my backpack, and wait patiently for the woman in front of me to finish buying a stack of clothes for her son, who slumps into the counter like someone sucker-punched him.

Dad wouldn't be able to stand the smell in here, but worse would be the sight of his daughter stealing. No matter why I wanted to go back to Rocky Hill, Dad wouldn't be right with this. He wouldn't want me to leave Mom, not for a weekend, not for a day.

And Mom? If she discovered me missing. . . . I couldn't do that to her.

But the price tag says $68. Plus tax. I'd love to tuck $70 in Mom's purse when she's not looking. I've seen her hunched over bills; I know it's not easy.

Sorry, Dad, I whisper, and put my not-best face to the world.

When the woman's done with her multi-bag purchase, I step up with the Abercrombie sweatshirt. I lay it on the counter and smile sweetly at the girl. "I have a return."

"Do you have a receipt?" she asks, staring somewhere past me, then suddenly at me.

"No," I say quickly, the ready lie spilling out. "My aunt gave it to me as a gift but she didn't give me a gift receipt."

The girl stifles a yawn. "I have to give you the sale price."

"I'm sure my aunt paid full price."

She shrugs. "Or store credit."

I snatch the sweatshirt off the counter. She flinches; her eyes, lined with blue-black, pop open wide.

"Never mind," I say, and stuff my arms into the sweatshirt. "I'll just keep it. Okay? Happy?"

Maddie

Lexi is sprawled on the porch swing with her friend Ted when I get home, her long tanned legs resting across his hairy ones. She's only three years older than I am, but she gets away with so much more. All I did was kiss Brendan, a boy I really like. She gets to drape herself all over Ted and nobody says a word. She says he's not her boyfriend, but judging by the moony look on his face, she forgot to tell him.

"How was the fashion show?" she calls out.

I ignore her.

Dad's in the backyard—technically, in the sandbox—with Scooter and Pete, getting buried in sand.

"Want me to bury you?" Pete asks me.

"No thanks, buddy." But I squat down and kiss the top of his head, then Scooter's. I would never tell them this, but I love their soapy, sweaty smell. A little bit baby, a little bit boy.

"How was school today, kiddo?" Dad asks. "Did the clothes work out?"

Mustering a smile, I hope that Dad won't notice my missing sweatshirt. "Yep, great. I'm doing a project on Emily Dickinson."

Lucky for me, Dad is preoccupied by being buried in sand. Plus, he told us last night that he got a new client. He's supposed to design a brochure for a company that makes a vitamin drink. After the boys went to bed, he began working on it.

When I ask Dad if I can go to Kate's to study math after

her practice, he says it's fine, as long as Kate's mom can give me a ride there and back, because he'll be bathing the twins. I rush inside, call Kate. She's already gone to practice, but her mom says it's fine.

At five thirty, Mrs. Miller's silver BMW glides into our driveway. "I know you girls have to study," she says after I've hopped into the back seat with Kate, who's still red-cheeked from practice, "but I need to run to the mall and get Aunt Sue a birthday present. Want to come along? You can study at the Starbucks."

The mall? Ugh. Yesterday's shopping was kind of fun; not so fun that I want to go back today. But we agree.

We trail behind Kate's mom at the mall, lugging our book bags past Build-A-Bear Workshop, Gap, and a store called Jungle Fashion that sells cheap clothes for old women—like Mom's age. Only Mom wouldn't be caught dead there. Her taste is plain yogurt.

At Starbucks we buy hot chocolate and cookies, and snag two plush armchairs wedged in the corner. After we devour the cookies and sip some of the scalding hot chocolate, we crack open our books to study the order of operations.

"Okay," Kate says. "What did Ms. Bonner tell us today about the order of operations?"

"She said to cut the foot off first?"

"Maddie."

"Um, you have to follow a special order?"

"Well, der. Which comes first? Puh . . . puh . . ."

"Parentheses?"

"Yes. Give the girl a cookie. So, you do the work inside the parentheses first. Then what?"

"I don't remember. Not at all. Not all, at all, at the mall, in the fall."

"Come on," Kate says. "You're not even trying."

A lady at the table next to us glances up, puts her finger to her lips and says, "Shush."

Kate whispers, "Okay, what next?"

"Addition and subtraction?"

Kate sighs. "Maddie."

After we have entered another fossil period, we're finished with our order-of-operations math packet and move on to the Emily D. report. I read aloud:

Much Madness is divinest Sense—
To a discerning Eye—
Much Sense—the starkest Madness—
'Tis the Majority
In this, as all, prevail—
Assent—and you are sane—
Demur—you're straightway dangerous—
And handled with a Chain—

"What the hay does that mean—'Much madness is divinest sense?'" Kate asks, twirling one of her corkscrew curls with her forefinger.

I chew on my pencil eraser and think. "I think she's saying so-called mad people can understand things other people can't, but so-called sensible people can believe things that are really crazy."

Kate's eyes glaze over. "And then," I say, snapping my fingers in front of her face, "she applies that to society. If you go along with the crowd you're considered really normal, but if you stand up for what you believe in . . ."

"Like Rosa Parks?"

"You'll be handled with a chain."

We high-five. Kate stares at me with wide-open eyes. "How did you ever get that?"

"How do you remember the order of operations?"

We laugh—loud—and Laptop Lady gets up, but not before shooting us a killer look. "Since when is Starbucks a study hall?" she says as she walks past us.

"Since when is it her home office?" Kate says, but only after she's long gone.

"Exactly. She should act like Emily Dickinson and write in her house. On little scraps of paper."

Kate shakes her head. "What a life. Wearing those long dresses. Never getting to play soccer."

"Can you imagine if Emily Dickinson was an eighth-grader?" I ask Kate.

"It'd be pretty tough," Kate says. "For her, I mean."

"Why?" I ask.

"Because she was a poet. And kind of a loner." Kate stares at me for a second. "Kind of like you."

"I'm not a loner," I say.

"Hey, don't get mad," Kate says. "It's a compliment. You don't need to have a million friends to make yourself look important."

"Well," I say, still mad, "I don't think Emily Dickinson was such a loner either. Remember that one poem?

Wild nights—Wild nights!
Were I with thee
Wild nights should be
Our luxury!

"I mean, who do you think she was writing that poem to? Her dog?"

Kate chuckles. She looks out into the mall. "Can you imagine Emily D. at a mall?"

"She'd probably run from store to store saying 'Wild bargains! Wild bargains!'" I say. We laugh hysterically until a brand-new adult slimes us with a look.

Before we can annoy any other Starbucks customers, Kate's mom swings by to pick us up, a shopping bag in her hand.

"Hey," Kate says to me as we're gathering up our stuff, "I've been meaning to ask you. How come no rec soccer? If you still want to play . . ."

"I found just the thing for Aunt Sue," Mrs. Miller chirps. "It's a lovely blue cashmere cardigan."

"I bet she'll love it," I say quickly.

"Yes, she has beautiful blue eyes, and this is exactly the right shade."

On our way to the parking garage, we pass by Jungle Fashion again. Kate grabs my arm and pulls me to a stop.

Jasmine

"'My life had stood a loaded gun,'" Tannis reads, jabbing at the Emily Dickinson poem as if she could force it to talk. "What does that mean?"

Mom leans over her shoulder. "Does she mean her life is like a loaded gun that hasn't shot anything yet?"

"Or is it more like she's writing from the point of view of a gun?" I ask. "See? She says, 'And now we roam in sov'reign woods, And now we hunt the doe—'"

Tannis's hot-pink fingernail traces down the poem. "Let's see if you're right—'I guard my master's head,' yadda yadda yadda, and the end. . . . 'For I have the power to kill, without the power to die.'"

"So it's a poem from the gun's point of view," Mom says. "Great."

"But it probably has some kind of hidden meaning," Tannis says. "That's why I hate poetry."

"But can't it mean what you want it to?" Mom asks me.

"Sure, if I want to get a C."

I glance up and see them coming: Kate, Maddie, and some preppy lady with her streaked blond hair in a ponytail.

I freeze, stare down at the page. It's too late to do anything, too late to take the sweatshirt off.

What if they come in here?

My heart gallops away.

Thief.

Yes.

Maddie

"Look," Kate says.

I look. Jasmine perches on a high stool next to the register counter. A book is spread out on her lap. A woman—maybe nineteen, twenty, or twenty-one—with brown highlighted hair, in skinny jeans and riding boots, is leaning over her shoulder, staring at the page. Behind the register a pretty woman with short hair stands ready to ring someone up.

But that isn't the most amazing part. Jasmine Princeton is wearing a maroon sweatshirt with giant Abercrombie letters across the chest. As soon as we get past Jungle Fashion, I catch Kate's shoulder to slow her down.

"Kate. Did you see what she was wearing?"

Under the glow of Karamel Korn, she shakes her head and her messy blond curls bounce all around.

"She's wearing a sweatshirt like mine."

Kate's fists curl up. "Let's go back and get it."

"Kate, no." I grab her arm. "She probably has one like it."

Mrs. Miller, several strides ahead of us, turns around.

"Come on, girls," she says. "I don't want to get stuck in rush-hour traffic getting home."

With one backward glance, I start walking again.

Kate's forehead creases. "But I thought you lost yours?"

"I did."

"She obviously took it."

I shake my head. "No, it's not possible. She wouldn't."

"Don't be naïve, Maddie. People steal stuff all the time."

"Even if she did *borrow* it," I say, "we can't march into Jungle Fashion and grab it."

"Why not?"

"Just because. I don't want to embarrass her."

"Have it your way. But you have to confront her tomorrow."

"Okay," I say quickly. Anything to stop talking about this.

By the dingy elevator to the parking garage, Mrs. Miller looks at me. "Everything okay, Maddie?"

I try for a smile. "I'm worried about surviving algebra. I hate math."

"Me, too." Mrs. Miller says. The elevator doors open, and she says, "Now where did I park that car?"

"J-14," Kate says, and Mrs. Miller chuckles.

"Do you remember the first time that happened?" Mrs. Miller asks me.

I've heard the story a million times, but I never get tired of it. Kate and I were four years old, and Mrs. Miller had brought us to Build-A-Bear Workshop. When it was time to leave, she couldn't remember where she had parked. A little voice piped out "A-17." That was Kate.

When we pull into my driveway, Mrs. Miller reaches back and pats me on the knee. "Don't be a stranger," she says.

Jasmine

Mom and Tannis close Jungle Fashion; Mom counts the drawer and fills out the daily cash report. She puts the cash and credit card receipts in the store's safe in the back for the manager to collect in the morning. Tannis and I check the dressing rooms and clean up the racks. The mall is quiet except for employees leaving, and the janitors, and the so-called flagship stores that stay open an extra hour. We grab pizza at the food court just before they close. As we gobble it down, Tannis tells us about her new boyfriend; Mom and I like the sound of him because he supports Tannis's dream of someday going to fashion design school.

After, Mom insists on walking Tannis to her car in the parking garage. In the shadows, I imagine rabid dogs growling, monsters staring, killers watching and waiting. I don't like parking garages at all. I don't like Mom and me out at night. I remember Dad telling me to keep an eye out for Mom, and I know what he meant. She's not as tough as us—as me.

"Bye, y'all," Tannis drawls as she climbs into her Mazda Miata.

"Tannis, you text me when you get home." Mom wags a finger at her.

"Okay, Mom," Tannis says, winking at me. But I think she secretly likes that Mom is keeping tabs on her. Tannis has been on her own since she was sixteen.

On the drive home, Mom blows a thin tendril of cigarette smoke out the window. She looks like a little kid smoking a cigarette.

"Do you want me to be an orphan?" I say. "Is that what you're trying to do here?"

"Jas," she sighs. "We've had this conversation too many times."

"But Mom. He died of friggin' cancer."

"It wasn't lung cancer."

I shake my head; try to snatch the burning cigarette. We swerve over the yellow line and back.

Mom straightens the wheel, hands me the cigarette. I stub it out in Ladybug's ashtray.

"Happy?" She raises an eyebrow.

"Yes." I laugh.

The road is empty; Mom and I are the only two people left in Connecticut. Ladybug follows the curve of the Merritt Parkway. We feel every little bump in the road but that's fine by me. I would miss Ladybug if we got another car. Besides, Ladybug is all we can afford.

Mom reaches behind her and presses her knuckles into the small of her back.

"My back . . ."

Headlights flood our car. My spine stiffens. A pickup

truck, higher than Ladybug, rushes up to us. Tailgates us.

Mom white-knuckles the steering wheel, even when a strand of her light brown hair falls right in her eyes. The blue light fills our car, rinses all the color from Mom's hair and skin.

The pickup rushes up, hangs next to us in the passing lane. The driver rolls down his window, yells something obscene.

"He's crazy." My voice shakes.

"Don't look, don't look," Mom urges me.

So I stare straight ahead.

Straight ahead.

Straight ahead.

Just us on the road and three exits to go.

Maddie

At dinner, Dad serves homemade mac and cheese and strawberry-rhubarb pie for dessert. Mom is home early enough to eat with us. She can't stop smiling. Her break from the world of magazine pre-publication is a pro bono client in Bridgeport. She found out that he had been awarded custody of his child, and his ex-wife, the drug-addicted mother of the child, was only allowed supervised visits.

"Sounds so sad," I say, helping myself to another scoop of mac and cheese.

"That's the real world, Maddie," Mom says quietly.

The implied criticism hurts, especially after Kate calling me naïve.

Later, finished loading the dishwasher, I run upstairs to my bedroom, claiming that I have to study algebra. I do, but I can't, so instead I flop on my bed and stare up at the white canopy. My racing thoughts lead me to knock on Lexi's door. She's been revising an essay for her AP History class, but she tells me to come in anyway.

"What should I do?" I ask, after I've explained about the sweatshirt.

"If you honestly think she took it, you have to talk to her. Confront her, Maddie."

That isn't what I wanted her to say; communist Lexi, I thought, would tell me it was only a fair redistribution of goods. Or something like that.

Back in my own room, the integers swim on the page like guppies. I pick up the biography of Emily Dickinson and read.

Jasmine

The pickup truck roars past, cuts right in front of us, then takes off.

"What a jerk," I say, turning to Mom, but I'm caught in the midst of my sentence by the tear sliding down Mom's cheek. She slaps it away angrily.

"Mom," I say, lightly putting my hand on her skinny, freckled arm.

"It's okay, baby," she says, as if I were the one who was crying. She sniffs a little, hiccups, and starts crying all over again. She hits the windshield wipers and they squawk across the glass.

"Hey, you're crying, not the car," I say. I know that doesn't make sense, but it makes Mom laugh and hiccup. She reaches into her purse and pulls out a pack of Kleenex. I see several—a dozen, even—packets of Kleenex. I breathe in softly.

We pull Ladybug into the Wishbone. Mom turns, takes my hands in hers.

"I can't protect you, Jas," Mom says. "From crazy people on the road. From that girl in Rocky Hill. From your dad dying." Her voice drops to a whisper. "What's going to happen to us, baby girl?"

"Nothing, Mom," I say firmly. "We're going to be fine."

"Of course we will, Jas. Of course." Her voice scratches out the words; her face, lit by the harsh yellow porch light, looks older to me, like it never has before. Faint lines etch the skin above her lips and spread from the corners of her eyes. Mom is working too hard, keeping us afloat. Why are we here in Clover? Why don't we move in with Uncle Louie? Or go home, back to Rocky Hill?

"But you can't keep working so hard, Mom. You're worn out. It's not good," I say.

"Jas, it *is* good. As good as it's going to get for now," Mom says. "I've got health insurance, dental, retirement."

"But the second job, Mom. I love Tannis, but . . ."

"I need that job to make ends meet, Jas," Mom says firmly.

If only I could work, hold down a job, help out.

Someday, I will. But what if it's too late?

We get out of the car, and as Mom is unlocking our door, I hear something. I glance over my shoulder. Through the space between two trailers, I can see over to the next row on the other side of the Wishbone. Sitting on the porch, lit by the porch light, his head on his knees, Ian is sobbing.

THURSDAY, SEPTEMBER 12

Maddie

How can I ask Jasmine if she stole my sweatshirt? I hurry down the hall, the stench of pine cleaner wafting off the floors, the lights a blur.

Jasmine rummages inside her locker, and she's wearing a brand new outfit—not the sweatshirt that's identical to mine.

"I saw you and Krater at the mall yesterday," she says over her shoulder.

"Kate? Her name is Kate. You were in that store."

Slamming her locker shut, she pivots. "How come you didn't come in and say hi?"

The morning bell rings and we walk together into the classroom. I breathe in the smell of pencils and Mr. Carty's coffee, take a deep breath so that I can say what I have to say. "Kate's mom was in a hurry. Why were you there?"

Her expression is neutral, gaze level. "My mom works there."

"Oh." Suddenly I'm on the defensive. "You were wearing my sweatshirt."

Her brow furrows. "What are you talking about? I got

that sweatshirt yesterday afternoon."

I spit out the words. "You bought one exactly like the one I lost? You really expect me to believe that?"

"I'm sorry you lost your sweatshirt, Maddie. But I really did get my sweatshirt yesterday. It was on sale at Abercrombie. Was yours on sale?"

I nod, my head weighing a ton.

"See?" she said. "Jesus, I can't believe you think I would take your sweatshirt."

"I know you took it," I mutter. "Just give it back."

Her eyes narrow. "No. I didn't. Say it again and I just might get mad."

I shake my head, blink angry tears, find my way to my desk blind.

The morning passes in a too-fast, too-slow blur of sonnets. Mr. Carty gives us a pep talk about Monday's Poetry Café and also about respectful listening and so on.

"Maddie," Mr. Carty says, "to get ready for the Poetry Café, we're going to decorate the library with the Warhol self-portraits you did in Art yesterday and put our 'I AM' poems underneath. Do you want the job? If so, pick someone to help you."

Normally I would love to be picked for something like this; today, however, I want to be invisible. Clearly I'm not, because I see Kate waving at me to pick her.

After we stop by the art room, Kate and I walk down to the library with a big roll of Andy Warhol self-portraits between us. We tape them on the blank wall that Mrs. Eilertsen has cleared for us. When we have them all up, we look them over.

"Maddie," Kate whispers. "She's wearing black in every single one. No smile. Depressing."

"She has a right to draw herself however she wants."

"She stole your new sweatshirt and you didn't say anything about it."

"I told you," I spit out. "I can handle it myself."

"Why don't you?"

We walk down the too-bright hall in silence.

After school, my brain is limp with facts. Waiting for the bus, I crane my neck and look at the sky plumped with clouds—the big fat marshmallow kind. I've always wanted to fly up and sit on one.

"Maddie?" Brendan's standing in front of me, grinning and following my gaze up to the sky. "What's so interesting up there?" he asks.

"Clouds," I say. Then, "I daydream a lot."

"So does my dad," Brendan says. "But he's an artist and he says it's part of the job description."

"Your dad is an artist?" I ask. "I thought he was, like, a banker or something."

"Yeah, well." Brendan looks down at the ground. "His bank tanked. So now he's pursuing his dream."

"My dad's an artist, too," I say. "And a graphic designer."

Brendan's smile widens. "I don't think I knew that. Hey,

anyway," he says quickly. "My dad and my little sister and I are going apple picking on Saturday. He said I could bring a friend and I was wondering. . . . Do you think your mom might let you go?"

I grimace. "My mom would say no. Nothing personal. She's just super protective. Very annoying."

He sighs but says, "My mom's like that, too."

"I read somewhere that killer whales stay awake for a whole month after their babies are born. I kind of think my mom is like that . . . you know, part killer whale."

Brendan grins. "It could be worse. She could be a kangaroo."

"Ew! What kind of apples are you getting?"

"Macouns. Those are the best. According to my dad. I'll bring you back one."

"Cool." Why do I sound so vocabulary-challenged?

He lopes off, whistling. Jasmine brushes by him, eyes fixed on me. I'd run away, but there's nowhere to go.

"Listen," she says. "It sucks that you lost your sweatshirt. I want you to take mine." Jasmine rummages in her backpack and pulls out a familiar maroon garment.

She drapes it around me.

"You've got to be kidding me!" I snatch the sweatshirt off my shoulders and wave it in front of her. "Do you think I'm an idiot?"

The bus rolls up with a screech of brakes. The driver opens the doors, and I climb on board, head to the middle, scoot in, and look out the window. In my peripheral vision I see Jasmine standing in the bus aisle, clutching her backpack to her chest.

"Can I sit with you?"

"No."

She slides in next to me anyway.

"I can't believe I was stupid enough to think . . ."

"Listen," she says, "I'm sorry. I was kind of cold, I saw this random sweatshirt on the floor. I picked it up. I was only going to borrow it. I didn't even know it was yours."

The bus starts up, pulls away from the curb.

"You saw me wearing the exact same sweatshirt in the morning. But even if I believed what you just said, why didn't you just tell me that in the first place?" I say. "Why did you make me feel like I had done something wrong?"

"You're right. I'm so sorry. I screwed up." There's something urgent in her voice, like she wants me to believe in her words, more than anything—like she wants to convince herself, too.

I look down at the heap of maroon in my lap. Look up at her and give a half-smile. The other half of this smile is stuck, though. I can't hide my feelings, because I've never been good at hiding anything. If Jasmine's so good at hiding whatever she doesn't want me or anyone else to see, how could I ever know if she's telling the truth?

"You're not going to forgive me, are you?" Jasmine looks down at her hands, her dark hair falling forward sudden as winter night.

"This stupid sweatshirt. I don't even care about it. My sister says I'm just a billboard for the company anyway. Here, keep it." I plop it into her lap.

She looks up. "I don't want it!" she says and tosses it back at me.

"No!" I toss it again and she throws back her head and laughs.

"No, thank you," she says firmly. She places it squarely on my lap. "It was dumb of me to pick it up and put it on. It was almost like I wasn't thinking. I just did it, and then . . . I don't know. Sometimes I just make dumb decisions."

"Me, too," I say. "Like, every day."

"Not every day," she says.

"Pretty much. Can we just forget about this wretched piece of maroon fabric?"

"Presto, change-o. Done," she says.

We pull up to Clover Elementary and the little ones climb on board. The girl who always sits with Jasmine scans the rows anxiously, then smiles when she sees her. "Jasmine!" she yells.

"Listen, I have to go sit with Breanna, and I know I'm not supposed to remember the wretched piece of maroon fabric"—she flashes her wild, beautiful smile—"but . . . can I make it up to you? I know you don't love math. I could come over and help you study."

"Now?"

Walking backward down the aisle, Jasmine ducks around fourth- and fifth-graders heading toward the back. "Why not?"

I give her a dorky thumbs-up. She plops down next to Breanna, who gives her a hug.

When we get to my stop, she ruffles Breanna's hair and follows me down the steps to my cute little cul-de-sac and my cute white house, which I'm suddenly seeing through her eyes. Jasmine, with her skinny black jeans and her cool black boots, with her swinging dark hair and deep purple shirt—she looks more like Soho should be her backdrop, not Clover's pompous colonials and boring, utterly predictable lawns. Does my street make me seem boring, too? I sigh and plow ahead; it's not like I can tear it down or paint it black.

In the backyard Scooter and Pete are drawing with chalk on the patio. They zoom up for a hug, covering me with chalk.

"I made a volcano that explodes," Scooter says.

"I made a fire truck to put out the fire," Pete says.

"But then there's another fire," Scooter adds. "It's bigger than Dad."

"These are my brothers," I tell Jasmine, rolling my eyes. "Twerps, this is Jasmine."

"Hi, guys." Jasmine high-fives them, and I can tell they are in love, preschool style.

"Wanna see my drawing?" Scooter says. He grabs Jasmine by the hand and pulls her over to the patio. Pete and I follow. She kneels down and points to one "interesting" thing about each of their drawings.

"Come on," I tell her, holding out my hand to pull her up.

"Jaswin," Scooter says. "Wanna see me draw T. Rex?"

"No, she doesn't," I say. "Come on, Jasmine. I know it may seem mean of me. But trust me, around here you've got to defend your territory."

Jasmine glances over her shoulder at them as I move us toward the door.

Jasmine

I say, "I wouldn't know. I'm an only child. I think they're cute."

I try not to get angry at Maddie when she complains about her brothers. I think about all that Maddie has, and doesn't realize that she has.

When Dad was dying of cancer, his skin puckered like Death Valley. Pun intended. We hovered over him like honeybees until he made us go away. Was he mad? That we were moist with good health and dumb with it?

I don't think so. Dad couldn't blame us for living, just like we couldn't blame him for dying.

But sometimes I think we all did get mad at each other.

I shouldn't fault Maddie for not knowing what loneliness feels like.

But I do.

Maddie

"Maybe they could go live with you for a week," I suggest to Jasmine as I hold open the French doors that lead to the kitchen.

She follows me, stepping gingerly, as if our floor might be made of quicksand.

Dad is pulling a tray from the oven. "Hi, sweetheart." He sees Jasmine. "Oh, hello. Meet to please you." Dad puts the tray on the stove, takes off his ridiculous lobster-claw potholders, sticks out his hand, and wiggles his eyebrows.

I'm in the process of succumbing to death by embarrassment, but Jasmine laughs and shakes Dad's hand.

After Jasmine texts her mom, we sit at the kitchen table, cracking open our math books. Dad sets a platter of oatmeal raisin cookies in front of us and then heads out the door with a paper plate of cookies for the boys.

"Inverse operations?" Jasmine asks, her mouth full of cookie.

"Um, operations that outdo each other," I say, taking a wild guess.

Jasmine smiles and shakes her head. "Undo. So, the inverse of addition?"

"Subtraction?"

"Right. Moving right along to the fundamental rule of algebra."

I scrunch my nose. "It's wretched?"

Jasmine laughs and a bit of cookie flies straight out of her mouth, onto my hand.

"Ew," I say, shaking it off.

"All right, sister, let's get serious before your dad makes me go home."

"As if. Then he'd have to help me."

"The fundamental algebra rule is . . . drum roll, please."

I give her a drum roll.

"What you do to one side of the equation, you have to do to the other side."

"Okay," I say. "That sounds easy, but it's never that simple."

Jasmine squishes a raisin between her thumb and forefinger. She pops it in her mouth. "Think of it this way," she says. "On one side of the equation there's . . . a guy who is handsome and smart, with two parents who love him. On the other side of the equation there's a guy who is handsome and smart, but he only has one parent. What do you have to do to make both sides equal?"

"Hmm. I think I know what you want me to say. Give one guy a parent, or kill one of the other guy's parents."

"Or make the guy with one parent fabulously wealthy," she says.

"Or the guy with two parents hideously ugly."

"With body odor."

Dad strolls in with Pete and Scooter. "You guys are making algebra look really fun," he says, over our snorting laughs. He drags the boys straight through to the rec room.

We snicker a few more times. Then I say, "I wish algebra was that fun."

"And I wish life was really that simple."

After we study for a while, my brain aches. "Let's go listen to music in my room," I say. We run upstairs, my feet barely touching the carpet.

Jasmine looks around the hallway. "Is your sister home?"

"She's at an Amnesty International meeting. Come look at her room." I open the door and we duck our heads in. Posters of Che Guevara and Mother Theresa cover two walls, and a third wall is a rich, dense green. Her ceiling is midnight blue, painted with tiny silver stars.

"Over the top, right?" I tap Jasmine on the shoulder. "Come on, let's go, in case she comes home. She's very temperamental."

Jasmine follows me down the hall. "Here's my room," I say.

Pink. Ever-loving pink. I give myself eyestrain trying to observe Jasmine's expression without actually looking at her.

"Nice," she says, looking around. "It's so big. And decorated. You have a real canopy bed."

"Perfect for a three-year-old, right?" I flop onto my bed to hide my embarrassment.

Jasmine moves to the window and fingers the frothy white-and-pink curtains that match my bedding. "It's so pretty," she says in a quiet voice.

I jump up and click on iTunes, letting the music change the subject. We listen as we paint our nails and braid each other's hair. Jasmine picks up a necklace that hangs from a sconce near my desk. I made it from a kit. It spells my name,

"Maddie." I used to be so proud of it. It was hard, in first grade, to figure out how to put the beads on right to spell my name correctly. It took me three tries.

Jasmine holds it between her long fingers. "It's sweet," she says.

"I'm not a big jewelry person," I say. I find myself telling her about Gram's emerald ring, and how my parents gave it to Lexi for her sweet sixteen.

I never saw Gram wear her emerald ring. When I asked her why, she told me her hands were too busy for rings. Busy pulling weeds, washing dishes, stirring her famous mulligan stew. And I was her girl, glued to her side when she came to live with us after the twins were born. Green-eyed, like her.

Jasmine says, "Seems a little unfair. Does your sister ever let you borrow it?"

"I've never asked."

When Jasmine leaves, she tells me that her mom is going to pick her up on North Avenue, the main road. "She's bad with directions," Jasmine explains.

I watch Jasmine through the living room window. When she reaches the end of the driveway, she turns and looks back—straight in my direction—before continuing onto North Avenue. A weird, sad feeling washes over me. Jasmine is good at hiding her emotions, so maybe I'm wrong when I see hesitation in her face. Is her mom really coming to pick her up? Did she even have permission to be here? I've never had a friend just come over unplanned and then leave without a parent.

In the kitchen Dad is playing The Beatles, loud. He turns it down when I come in. The twins are in the family room, watching *Thomas & Friends.*

"When's dinner?" I ask.

"Nice to see you, too," he says. He hands me a stack of plates from the cupboard to set the table.

"Sorry, Dad. I'm starving. Jasmine stuffed my brain with math facts." I put out all the plates and go back for the silverware.

"How come Kate didn't come, too? She's good at math." Dad chops veggies at the speed of light.

"Have you ever thought of having your own cooking show?" I ask, nudging past him for the water glasses.

"Did you hear my question?"

"Dad, I have more than one friend."

"I know. But while you're making new friends, don't forget about the old ones, too. You know what I mean?" Dad breaks into song. *"Make new friends, but keep the old. One is silver, the other is gold."*

I clap. He takes a bow. Then I say, "I know, Dad. But Jasmine and Kate . . . don't really get along."

Dad frowns. I'm putting the forks on top of the napkins when Lexi whips through the door. Scooter and Pete race in from the family room, tackling Lexi with hugs.

"Boys, get off your sister," Dad calls. "Go wash up. Time for dinner. Welcome home, Comrade."

Scooter knocks into me and I almost drop a water glass.

"Hey, Dad. Hey, Maddie-lu," Lexi says. "How was school?"

"Delirious," I say. "Math is horrible."

She grabs a banana out of the fruit bowl and peels it.

"We're about to have dinner," Dad protests. "Stir fry."

Lexi grins. "I'll still be hungry." She eats half of the banana in one bite. "Need help studying?"

"I studied with Jasmine."

Lexi finishes the last bite of her banana. "You invited her over? But you thought she stole your sweatshirt."

Dad drops his chopping knife. I've finished setting the table and all I want to do is get out of the kitchen. But Dad raises his hand, as in, "Oh, no, you don't."

"What is this about a sweatshirt?" he says.

"Nothing," I say. "If Lexi would open her eyes, she'd see that the sweatshirt is draped right on that kitchen chair."

Lexi grabs me by the arm as I try to snake around her and wags her finger in my face. "You thought she stole it. You were *positive*."

I detest my sister. Did I not tell her this in the privacy of her bedroom? "So? Clearly I was wrong."

"Why is your face beet red like it gets when you're lying?"

I shove her. "No, it's not," I brilliantly retort.

"Girls!" Dad slaps his lobster-claw oven mitt on the counter. "Stop it. Mom is going to be home any minute now. Maddie, if you're in the mood for fighting, go to your room until dinner."

"Why do I always get the blame? What about her?"

Dad points to the stairs. I stomp up to my room. I loathe my family. Loathe!

And I miss Gram, who never blamed me for anything, told me I was "perfectly Maddie" and said "Who could ask for anything more?" I want to see her with her glasses taped together from where she sat on them and wouldn't let Mom get her another pair. I want to see her rescuing stray cats, writing to our congresswoman, making wild desserts on Wednesdays. *Just because,* she said when Mom scowled her *Whys*.

On the top stair, my bare toes curl into the soft white carpet. What would Gram think if she knew Mom and Dad gave her ring to Lexi? I'm electrified and dangerous, like one of those crazy metal fences I saw once at a dude ranch on a family vacation. That ring will never be mine, thanks to my parents. But I'm sure that wasn't what Gram wanted.

I listen for a moment, then I hear from downstairs the ripple of my sister's laugh, exuberant, alive, wrapping someone—Dad? the boys? a friend on the phone?—in her Lexiness.

I walk straight to her door, snap it open, and barge in. The jewelry box sits primly on her night stand. I open it up, try on the ring. It sparkles, like afternoon sun on a dark green leaf.

"Dinner," Lexi calls from downstairs.

I slip the ring in my pocket. I'll wear it tomorrow for good luck on the math test. Then I'll put it back. She'll never even notice it's missing. Somewhere in the universe, are Gram's green eyes gazing on my ring-grazing? Does she see me, thief girl, barefoot and cautious as a cat?

Jasmine

The bus route from Maddie's house to the Wishbone is pretty straightforward. Not so hard. I got a good sense of direction from Dad, he claimed, but I always thought I got it from Mom. She got us from New Hampshire to Clover with no GPS, like they have in new cars. Least I can do is navigate a few lousy streets.

I pass by one lonely house after another, their windows blinded with curtains. Nobody's pulling weeds, no kids doing cartwheels across the lawn. Not even a single dog moseys down the street. Where are the barbecues and hula hoops? Where are the teenagers biking home one-handed 'cause they've got a box of pizza in the other hand? Where are the old ladies watering begonias at dusk?

We're on a desert island, I complain to Mom. But she says we're in a genteel New England town where people mind their manners and keep their dogs inside electric fences. Indy wouldn't have liked that.

A rottweiler suns himself in his yard. He looks up when I walk by, then gives a deep, throaty bark. He hoists himself up and ambles over. I stop walking, turn, and hold my hands out. "Hey, there," I say softly to him. "You're a nice boy?"

He licks my hand. I wish I had a treat for him. A dog cookie or a piece of hamburger. I wonder if the Grays are treating Indy okay. I wonder if they let him sleep on the bed, under the covers, like I did.

I scratch the dog under his chin, say goodbye, carry my feet toward Post Road. There I take a left, past a Dunkin' Donuts, a dry cleaners, a lady's clothing store, an antique store. WE BUY ANTIQUE JEWELRY, a sign in the window says.

The traffic comes at me in streams until one noisy, clanking car slows down, pulls over in front of me. With one hand, I check that my cell phone is in my back pocket. On my other hand, I twirl my turquoise ring with my thumb, then clench a fist. The window cranks down and it's Ian, sticking his head out. I breathe again, walk up warily, and peer into the car. He leans back and Mr. Albert leans forward.

"Hey, there, Jasmine. We saw you walking. Can we give you a lift?"

"Okay," I say and climb into the back seat, knowing all the while that Mom would kill me if she knew I was climbing into a stranger's car. Mr. Albert isn't quite a stranger, but almost. I hold my breath against the stale smell of beer.

"So, where were you coming from?" Mr. Albert says at the stop light. I see my forehead in the rearview mirror.

"Friend's house," I say. I blurt out, "You guys look so much alike."

Mr. Albert laughs. "My best piece of poetry." Ian sinks down in his seat just a little. Mr. Albert's face tightens. "What's the matter with you, kid? Can't you say something to your friend? Aren't you both in the same grade?"

"Hi," Ian mumbles.

Mr. Albert swats him on the arm, and my fists clench. "We're not in the same class," I say quickly.

The trailer court is just up ahead, past Willows Pediatrics and Post Road Animal Hospital. Mr. Albert turns in and parks, gives me a little salute. He walks off to their unit.

"You have a dad and no mom," I blurt out. "And I have a mom and no dad."

Ian throws me an angry look. "I have a mom. Who told you that? Bre?"

I flush, bite the inside of my cheek. "I meant, she's not around. Never mind."

"Good idea," he says. "Mind your own business. And next time my dad offers you a ride, do me a favor and say no."

Inside my quiet house, I crack open my math book, slam it shut, and fling it across the room. It smashes into the blank white wall and falls to the ground with a thud.

Loud, but not loud enough to chase the quiet away. Three hours and Mom will be home. I turn on the TV and laughter fills the room.

Maddie

At night, I dream of Gram's face next to mine, putting me to sleep with a bedtime story. Cobweb of time fanning across her cheeks. The gift of her hoarse voice, her minty breath.

But Gram is silent.

"Tell me a story, Gram." I plead.

"It's your turn to tell the story," she says.

Jasmine

At night, I dream of Dad, across the black railroad bridge. The water churns below.

"I'm afraid," I say.

He puts out a hand. I think to beckon me. I think to hold my hand. But no, it's palm out, to stop me.

"You're going the wrong way," he says.

FRIDAY, SEPTEMBER 13

Maddie

"Maddie," Mr. Carty calls.

I snap alert, swing like a dinghy back to the moment. Does Mr. Carty know I haven't been reading? Of course he knows. I can fool the Spanish teacher, the Art teacher, the Social Studies teacher. I can definitely fool the Social Studies teacher. Mr. Carty, however, has extra spacing-out perception. Four times he's reeled me back in when I'm swimming out in airhead ocean.

Today, though, he motions for me to come up to his desk, where our poetry journals tower in two stacks. I hurry up, stand there feeling the eyes of the class on me.

"I read your poem on the wall of the Poetry Café. Is that the one you're planning to read on Monday night?" he asks quietly. "Not your poem about your sister or some of the others you've written?"

"I don't know, Mr. Carty," I say, equally quiet. It's bad enough to be standing up here in front of the class.

"I have to admit I'm disappointed with the one on the

wall. It's . . . maybe not as original as some of your others?"

"I did my best," I protest.

"'I am a cupcake, dotted with sprinkles'?"

Harsh. But . . . I know he has a point. "I did a different one, but I didn't want to hang it up."

Mr. Carty makes a bridge of his fingertips. "Fair enough."

I smile, big-teeth style.

"If you agree to read a different poem at the Café."

My smile sags. "Do I have to?"

Mr. Carty leans forward. "Maddie, you have talent. Don't throw it away. "

I nod, glancing out at the classroom to see if anyone heard that.

"So you'll read a real poem at the Café?"

I have a blurt moment. "Mr. Carty, no one is taking this Café thing seriously. I don't want to be the only one who's up there spilling out her innermost feelings."

He makes a bridge of his fingers again. "You have a good point. Okay."

I sigh and take my seat, wondering what that means.

Mr. Carty says, "All right, people, our Poetry Café is this Monday. Maddie and I were just discussing which one of her fantastic poems she'll read." If I had only known that Mr. Carty planned to execute me by lethal praise, I would have carried a shovel to school today. To bury myself.

About forty-six eyeballs swivel toward me. I closely examine the scratches on my desk.

"Fantastic, you say," Mr. Carty continues. "Why fantastic? Because Maddie's poems are heartfelt. She uses real emotions as the raw materials of her . . . better poems. Each one of you has the same raw material and many of you have already written poems that are honest, or funny, or even heartbreaking. I'm going to hand back your journals. If I wrote 'DD' in pencil, it means I want you to try to dig deeper. And for the Poetry Café, if you want to read a poem that I've marked 'DD,' then you'll need to revise it, digging deeper, first."

He jumps up, grabs a stack of journals, and starts handing them back.

Everyone groans. Not me. To groan you must have breath, and I am deceased. Yes, no longer among the living.

After, at my locker, Sarah and Mikayla walk up to me. "Thanks a lot for the extra work, Double-D," Sarah says. "What does that stand for? Dum Dum?"

Jasmine circles around from the other side of me. "Are you that stupid?" she says to Sarah, lightly punching her on the arm and simultaneously gracing her with a brilliant smile. "Back to kindergarten for you. Besides, Maddie rocks for being an excellent poet, don't you think?"

Sarah flushes, stammers a "yes," walks away with Mikayla trailing behind.

Oh. My. Llama. My eyes wide, I say, "Thanks."

Jasmine shakes her head. "You, my friend, have *got* to learn to stick up for yourself."

"Easier said than done."

"Okay, first off, that's a cliché, and you're not allowed. Second, you have to work at it, Maddie. Like anything. And maybe it's not so easy for you, but you can't let that be an excuse, you know."

I pass a hand over my eyes, not because she's wrong. Not even because I don't want to be told this. But because she's taking the time to notice that I am standing here in this hall, in this school, in this town, on planet Earth.

She takes hold of my hand. "Shut up! Your sister let you borrow her ring?"

"Yeah, she did," I fabricate. *Fabricate* sounds better than *lie.*

"Cool!" Jasmine smiles at me approvingly. "That was really nice of her, no?"

The second bell rings, saving me from having to add new details to my lie.

In algebra, Ms. Bonner hands out our tests. I flip mine over and stare at all the order of operations problems and the emerald ring feels like a curse on my finger. I can't remember anything after doing the problem inside the parentheses first. Beyond that, snapping integer crocodiles swim through the murky swamp that is my "math brain." I have no idea what I'm doing, but I'm fairly certain my answers are wildly, amusingly incorrect.

I want to whine to Kate after Algebra, but she sprints out of the classroom, trying to catch up with some guy in a Red Sox hat.

At lunch, I get my food and then I look for Kate and find her just coming out of the line, already talking and joking with Aaliyah. She sees me, holds her tray with one hand, and waves, making her way over to me.

"Hey, Kate," I say with a large smile. It just feels toothy, like I'm baring my teeth to a predator. People swarm around us, knocking into us a little as we step to the side, by the juice and water machine.

She gestures toward the soccer table. "Come sit with us." Apparently, it's her new table. I knew this day would come, but still, I am not ready for it. My head is buzzing.

"I can't do that."

"Why not?"

"Because only *you* want me to be there. Not them. It'll be awkward, you know?"

Kate's gaze shifts from me to them. "I don't know why you're creating such a drama about this. It's just lunch. What am I supposed to do?"

"I think you already made up your mind about that." And I start to turn away.

"Maddie!" Kate calls out. "This is not my fault, so stop acting like it is."

"It's not your fault. But it is your choice."

"But they're my friends, too! Am I supposed to only be friends with you? That's not fair." Kate stops short. "I'm sorry, Maddie." She puts her hand on my shoulder.

"You're right," I say, and my voice is lower, softer now. "It's not fair. I get that. And I get that you want to sit with them. Go ahead and we'll catch up later."

"Are you sure?"

"Speaking of brown dogs sure."

But when I turn away from Kate, I let my lips stop smiling. I let my eyes find a far spot in the cafeteria and I stare at it, and keep staring the whole while I thread through the lunchroom until at last I can sit.

Jasmine plunks down across from me. "I have a question for you. I'm wondering if you want to trade." Jasmine holds out her hand. She has a pretty turquoise ring on her one finger. "For a day. My mom and dad gave me this ring for my birthday last year."

"It's really pretty."

She holds it, turns it this way and that. A look crosses her face—a memory that pulls in her eyes. "My dad got it in the Army, when he was stationed in New Mexico. He gave it to my mom for their engagement before he could afford a real diamond." Her fingers fly to her lips, as if to put the words back.

"You shouldn't lend it to anyone," I say, chiding her, but gently.

"Just for a day."

"It's a beautiful ring, Jasmine. But I can't. I have to put this ring back before my sister notices it's gone."

Jasmine raises an eyebrow. "I thought she lent it to you."

My ears get hot. "Not exactly." I notice an ant crawling up the wall. Pete told me ants can crawl up walls because they have special sticky pads called arolia. Lucky ant. I wish I could crawl away, too. "Sorry, I . . . can't."

"Okay, I understand. You took it without asking."

She laughs, a mocking sound, then scrapes back her chair without another word.

The room hums with words. They buzz and crackle, burst into roars. Teeth clacking, lips licking, chairs scraping forward and back.

No one can hear my raw, shallow breaths. Not even me.

By the end of the day, I'm leaning into my locker, hoping the cold metal will ease my throbbing head, when Jasmine walks by me on her way to her locker.

"Hey, Jasmine," I call out.

She pretends not to hear me.

My stomach twists; will I always be as alone as I am in this minute? Maybe I'm meant to be a single integer, subtracted down to one. The Jasmine lifeline floats away, leaving me treading water.

"Want to trade?" The hall's fluorescent lights burn my head. My desperate question hangs in the air.

She turns; her eyebrows arch. "Trade?"

"You know, like you said before. Your ring and my ring. For the weekend."

Jasmine slams her locker shut and turns toward me, considering. She stares to some distant point, and the moment stretches on and on like a rubber band. Snap, she's back, a slow smile lighting her face. In a few quick moves, she's at my side, throwing her arms around me. "Sure," she says. "I'll do it."

Yanking Lexi's emerald ring off my finger, I hold it out to Jasmine and she slides it on. She stares at it for a long time, then she slips her own ring off and hands it to me. I put it on. It feels like a scab on my skin.

My whole body feels that way.

Itching and burning. And my stomach turns over and over.

Jasmine

When Maddie asks me if I want to trade, I remember: Driving home, Dad and Mom started arguing about something. He pulled over to the side of the road, got out, and took off on foot. She went to follow him but fell onto the gravel, hands down. He came running back down the road. His face was twisted. "Baby, are you hurt?" he kept saying, cradling her in his arms and picking gravel from the pads of her hands. "I'll never leave you, I promise." I watched the whole thing, and I believed him.

But that was a lie. She needs him now, and he's gone. And I'm the one in charge. I'm the one who's supposed to take care of her. This ring could keep that promise. Couldn't it, Dad?

Maddie

As I begin to walk home from the bus stop, my head pulses, like my heart moved inside it. I'm shivering and sweating, dizzy, and the ground feels like it's a million miles away.

Jasmine

The school bus turns the corner. It's zipping by Dunkin' Donuts and the consignment store, when I yell, "Stop!"

The driver glances in the rear view mirror.

"Kid, I can't stop," he hollers.

"But I want to get out here," I say.

"Well, too bad," he says. "So sit down, now."

Breanna twists around in her seat. "Why're you being bad?" she whispers.

I grin at her. "I'm not being bad. I just had an idea."

"About what?"

"How to help my mom."

Breanna brightens up. "You going to get her some doughnuts?"

The bus pulls up to the Wishbone.

We climb off, first Breanna, then me, then Ian.

"No, not doughnuts," I tell her.

She grins up at me. "Too bad. She'd like some doughnuts."

I laugh. "Oh, she would, would she?"

Breanna smiles wide.

"Hey," I say. "You lost another tooth."

"C'mon," Ian says, pushing her along.

"Ian," I call after him.

He keeps walking down the skinnybranch-littered road.

I rummage in my backpack. It's broken in half, but it should still work.

"Ian!" I yell again. This time he stops. I sprint forward,

smack a Hershey's bar into his hand.

"What's this?" he says.

"A Hershey's bar," Breanna and I say at the same time.

"I'm sorry," I say, just me. And I mean, *for everything.*

"This is you minding your own business?" he asks, but with a smile.

"That's about right." I grin back.

I watch them walk home, past the rough-skinned cottonwood trees, and smile a little to myself at the thought of Ian and me, friends. Dad would be happy. He said some people can't see past the surface. All they see is skin or weight or clothes.

Funny. I forgot he ever said that.

I touch the ring, twist it right, then left.

What would you say if you knew? Is it a Robin Hood move? Steal from the rich, give to the poor?

Or is it just plain stealing?

You're not around to ask, so leave me alone.

I walk, then run home, fast as I can. The door sticks like it wants me to reconsider. Finally get it open, fling my backpack inside, check my phone; Mom's text says she's heading to Stop & Shop before she comes home.

That decides it.

Maddie probably has a bank account deep as a well. If she knew the good I could do for my mom, she'd want me to use this ring to do it. That's what she'd say, if she knew.

Maddie

Dad carries me up to my room. Scooter and Pete run after us. It must have scared Pete when I fainted on the patio because he's still crying hard. He follows Dad and stands outside my door.

"It's okay," I say to him. But I don't feel okay.

Dad hurries to get the thermometer, and I take off my clothes in a daze, put on my pajamas, and slide between my cool sheets. Before he returns, I fall into a deep sleep. When I wake up, the air is hot and heavy and thick. My stomach feels as if I've stepped off a stair I didn't see coming.

I barely make it to the bathroom before I throw up all over the floor. "Dad," I call weakly from the door.

He runs up the stairs, taking two at a time. "It's Betty Barfy," he jokes. I throw up again. By the time I make it back to bed, my stomach hurts and my throat burns. I fall asleep and wake up minutes—hours?—later. Through my open door, I hear Mom and Dad talking in the hallway in low voices.

"Mom," I croak.

"Oh, honey, you're awake." Mom rushes over and sits on the edge of my bed. Her large hazel eyes have shadows underneath. She puts her cool hand on my forehead. "I think your fever is down. How do you feel?"

"Thirsty."

Mom runs to get me some water and then props me up in bed with some pillows. I drink down some huge gulps even though Mom tells me not to.

"Where's everybody else?" I say weakly.

"The boys are sick," Mom says. Her voice sounds like it's carrying a thousand tires or a million bricks. "Dad is in there with them."

"Oh, no," I say. I swallow hard. "I'm sorry, Mom."

Mom sighs and brushes back a lock of hair. "It's not your fault."

But I do feel bad. Nobody should be nice to me. I took my sister's ring. Gram's ring. How could I have done that? What was I thinking? What if Jasmine loses it? I want to get up and IM her. Tell her I need the ring back. Can't possibly wait another second.

JaSMiNe

Now is my moment. The door jangles when I open it, a whole bunch of bells. Mom told me that a jewelry store owner had been shot to death in Fairfield. I don't blame this lady for being careful. Still, even when I give her my best smile, the one that always gets people to smile back, she only looks at me over her half-glasses. "Can I help you?" she says, in a voice that sounds like *What do you want?*

"Um, I have something I was wondering if you could sell for me. Like you'd take a . . ."—what should I call it? A commission? A percentage? I should have thought this through more—"a percentage," I settle on.

"What do you have in mind?" she asks, folding her red silk–covered arms across her chest.

"I have a ring," I say.

She motions for me to come forward, so I do. Then I lay my hand on her freshly Windexed counter. Her nose wrinkles a little as she glances down. The emerald ring, surrounded by tiny white diamonds, glows its deep rich green.

Her face doesn't change expression. She asks to see it. When I take it off, she holds it up to the light. She weighs it and examines it through a magnifier. All the while I'm trying to keep my expression as still as hers, to press my toes into the floor and stay steady. "Where did you get this ring?" she asks.

"My grandmother gave it to me."

"Then why are you bringing it to me?"

I decide to aim for close to the truth. A version, anyway. "She left the ring to me when she died. I could use the money. You know, to buy new clothes, presents for my mom."

The woman studies me for a long minute. "I'd like to sell it for you," she says, "but first I'd need a parent to accompany you. I can't just sell it without some kind of written consent."

"But why?" I hear the desperation in my voice. I can tell she hears it, too.

"To verify ownership, for one. And until then," she says, "I'm going to hold this ring for you."

She hands me a claim check and puts the emerald ring in a baggie.

"Please give it back to me," I say.

"I'm sorry," she says. "I'm sure you understand."

"You can't do that." God, I hate how scared my voice sounds.

She opens a file cabinet and tosses the ring in. "I just did."

I bang on the glass counter, and she jumps back. "Please, you don't understand. I need the money for my mom."

She puts her hand on the phone. "Get out of my store now, or I will call the police."

"I'll come back with my mom, and you're going to be sorry." Will she believe Tannis is my mom?

As I turn to leave, she says, "I drive by you every day on my way to work. You're one of those trailer-court kids. Do you honestly think I would just take something from you with no questions asked? This is a consignment store, not a pawn shop."

I do exactly what I did the first time I saw her stare. Flip her off. But this time I make sure she sees.

SATURDAY, SEPTEMBER 14

Maddie

Mom keeps coming in and out of my room, bringing me chicken broth and crackers. She's looking really tired, and I tell her I'm fine taking care of myself. She should help Dad with the boys. We can both hear that isn't going too well. Scooter is bawling his eyes out.

"I don't like throwing up," I can hear him crying from all the way down the hall. Poor Pete probably feels as bad, but he's a whole lot quieter.

I doze off and when I wake up in the afternoon, I'm better—but Mom, Dad, and Lexi are *all* throwing up. Mom is too sick to worry about everyone else, which is good.

The boys need to get some liquids down or they'll get dehydrated; coaxing them to drink is surprisingly easy. They're thirsty and by late in the day Scooter is complaining loudly that he's hungry. A good sign.

"There's barely any food in the house," Mom groans. "What are we going to do?"

"I know," I say to Mom and Dad at their bedroom door.

"I'll call up that grocery delivery service and order the BRAT diet. Perfect for them."

"Very funny," Dad says weakly. But he smiles with his eyes closed.

I call the service and order bananas, rice, applesauce, and bread for toast. Before you can say "BRAT," the boys are munching bananas and applesauce in bed. I read them some books and they watch a dinosaur show.

When I come back upstairs, Mom and Dad are sitting up in bed. Mom's smartphone is blinking and vibrating like a little space creature. I bring them Maddie's Stomach Bug Special and they take a few sips of water, although Dad doesn't look so good after he drinks his. Mom wants to get out of bed and check on the boys, but I won't let her.

Her eyes well with tears. "I'm so proud of you, Maddie. You're really doing a great job helping us."

"Mom," I say. "I'm not two." But secretly I'm proud of myself, too.

I hear groans from Lexi's room and dash off to check on her. Miss Twenty Friends doesn't look so hot. In fact, you might say she looks gross. Her blond hair is all stringy and her normally glowing skin is more like gray construction paper.

"Leave me alone," Lexi moans.

"You have to keep a little water down," Mom calls.

Uh-oh. Lexi is a terrible sick person. She turns into a vicious dingo.

"I said, leave me alone!" she screams.

"You have to drink, you idiot." I hand her the water cup. She takes a drink. Throws it up into her waste basket.

"Thanks a lot," she moans.

"Alexis Grace," Mom calls from the other room. "Your sister is only trying to help you."

Lexi flops back in bed.

"Try again," I say.

She shakes her head.

"Come on, Lexi. Take a sip. Or you'll get dehydrated."

"Not yet," she groans. "I'll throw up . . ." She looks at my hand. "Where did you get this ring?"

"From Jasmine."

"She gave it to you?"

"Yeah." My face breaks out in a cold sweat.

Before Lexi goes back to sleep, she mumbles, "Thank you for taking care of me. You're a good sis."

Ugh. Mother Teresa in the poster on Lexi's wall is giving me a dirty look. *It's people like you who keep me busy!*

Calm down. You'll get the ring from Jasmine on Monday.

In my room, I send her a quick text: *I need ring back ASAP. K?*

Her reply: *We traded.*

JaSMiNe

Reading her text, I almost vomit.

SUNDAY, SEPTEMBER 15

Maddie

Mrs. Sweeney, who sometimes babysits the twins, comes over to help since Mom and Dad are still in recovery mode upstairs. Likewise, Lexi. While Mrs. Sweeney's checking up on the twins, I grab the school directory and look up Jasmine. There she is: Jasmine Princeton, 1200 Post Road East. I stare at the address, chewing my lip. Post Road is all businesses, so that can't be right, unless Jasmine lives at Dunkin' Donuts. I try looking in the White Pages online. There's a Donald Princeton in Milford and a Robert Princeton in Danielson. But nobody in Clover. I have no choice but to try 1200 Post Road East.

With the address tucked into my pocket, I put on my sneakers and ask Mrs. Sweeney if I can go for a bike ride. Mrs. Sweeney looks up from Candy Land, which she's playing with Scooter and Pete. "What do your parents say?" she asks in her Lucky Charms Irish accent.

"They say as long as I stay on our street."

"All right then. Wear your helmet, dear."

"Can I go, too?" Scooter asks. "Please."

"No."

Hopping on my bike, I peddle down to the main road, North Avenue. One SUV after another roars past, plus some trucks. In a ten-second pause in the traffic, I push my bike across the street, and on the other side, I stop. Maybe because I've been sick, I'm out of breath. I'm leaning against my bike, gasping, when I hear a little voice calling my name.

"Maddie. Maddie!"

I turn around. Beyond the speeding cars, Scooter sits on his tricycle, at the very edge of the street.

"Scooter!" I scream. He bursts into tears. "It's okay," I call. A huge truck whistles by, blowing my hair back.

"I want to come wiff you." He pedals forward, right into the street.

"No, Scooter!" I yell. "Get back! Now!" He stops. "I'm coming to you. Stay right there, okay? Okay, Scooter?" I drop my bike in the grass. He nods, sniffling. A white SUV hurtles down the road and swerves to the other lane when the driver sees Scooter by the side of the road. What if the next driver hits him? Fast as I can, not daring to look, I run, past black and silver and a car horn that blasts and blasts again. But I make it to Scooter. I fall to my knees and hug him. Hug him and hug him and smell his funny baby-shampoo and applesauce and dirt smell.

"Are you mad at me?" he says, his voice all wobbly.

"No, Scooter." How can I be mad at him? I'm supposed to set a good example, and here I am, biking on North Avenue. Mrs. Sweeney probably thought it was fine for him to ride his tricycle in the driveway since I was supposed to be out there, too, biking up and down the short cul-de-sac. I take Scooter's grubby little hand and we trudge up the road, with me bent over, pushing his tricycle in front of us. I can barely make my legs move; all my muscles have turned to pudding.

When we reach the driveway, as gently as possible I say, "Scooter, you can never, ever come down to North Avenue, do you understand me? You need to be with Mommy or Daddy."

His mouth trembles again. "Okay."

"Scooter, let's make it a secret, okay? I won't tell if you won't tell."

Mrs. Sweeney rushes out of the house, holding Pete's hand, calling "Scooter! Where are you, Scooter?" Poor little Pete is sobbing. Mrs. Sweeney doesn't look so good, either.

"Here he is!" I call out, fake-cheerful. "I forgot to ask if Scooter could come with me up and down the block," I lie. "I'm so sorry, Mrs. Sweeney. I didn't mean to scare you."

Mrs. Sweeney puts her hand on her chest. "I think that's enough excitement for my ticker." She pats her heart. "Why don't you come inside now, boys? Let your sister go for a bike ride." She peers at me. "Where is your bike, Maddie?"

"Over there," I mumble, pointing over my shoulder.

She nods. "We'll play another game of Candy Land, okay, boys?"

"Okay. I don't want a truck to run me down," Scooter says.

Never trust a four-year-old with a secret. It's like asking them to guard a Snickers bar. Luckily, Mrs. Sweeney doesn't seem to hear him. "I can't wait to get to Candy Cane Forest," she says, grabbing each of them by the hand.

And I take off. This time, nothing's going to stop me. Not even a pit of molasses.

After about five minutes of truck wind, the traffic finally lets up enough for me to cross North Avenue and grab my bike, still lying in the grass. I pedal down the sidewalk, zipping by dogs barking in their yards, the high school where boys are shooting hoops. Turn right onto Long Lots Road, past the grand old homes, cross it, and zip straight down Pumpkin Hill Road. It's like a ski slope. *Whee!* I take a left on Morningside and at the bottom I'm on Post Road. The traffic is thick and fast, like ketchup that spurts out of the bottle. *Gulp.* Mom will kill me if I get killed.

There's a sidewalk for this part of Post Road. I steer onto it, passing a busy Starbucks, a tire store, a bike store, an ice cream store, and a diner where my family eats sometimes.

Ten minutes of hard biking brings me to 1200 Post Road East. My heart thunks away. The perfectly paved trailer court, edged in rhododendrons, is like a mini-town, with every house exactly like the next one. But which one is Jasmine's? The address in the school directory didn't include a house number. How am I going to find her?

At the first trailer, a young woman is planting fall mums into a container. She looks up at me and smiles. Two boys wheel around on trikes, making a figure-eight pattern.

"Hi," I say. "Do you guys know Jasmine?"

They stop and straddle their trikes, stare at me.

"I do," one says. "She gave me a lucky penny."

"So do I," the other one says. "But I never got one."

"She lives right there," the first one says, pointing. "I'm four and three-quarters."

"I'm his brother, and I'm three and five-quarters," the second one says. "Pets aren't allowed. But we have a cat anyway." He glances at his brother, who scowls at him.

I smile a little. "I won't tell."

Hopping on their trikes, they wheel away. I watch their figure eight for a second before turning toward Jasmine's house. My palms go all sweaty. What am I doing? The bike's kickstand folds, and my bike crashes to the ground. A curtain flicks open, snaps shut. I drag myself up to the front step, and before I can ring the bell, the door swings open. A woman in a man's plaid robe that is way too big for her smiles at me.

"Hi, sweetie. Can I help you?" she asks.

I open my mouth to say something, but no words come out.

"Can I help you?" she repeats, her round blue eyes widening a bit.

"Mom," a voice calls out. "Who is it?" Jasmine's voice.

She squints at me. "You okay, sweetie? Are you lost?"

Jasmine's head pops over her Mom's shoulder. The skin around her lips goes white; her nostrils flare.

"Jasmine told me she was going to have a friend come over one of these days. Jasmine, why didn't you remind me last night?" Her mom opens the door wide. "Come in, honey."

Careful not to look at Jasmine, I follow her mom into a kitchen that smells like Ajax and sugar. Jasmine and I sit at the table while her mother pulls plastic wrap off a plate. Jasmine traces a floral pattern on the tablecloth, around and around and around.

"This is temporary," she says in a low voice. "Until my mom can choose a real house."

I nod and steal a look at Jasmine's hand. No ring. Maybe she has it stored somewhere.

"Have some cookies," Jasmine's mom says. She slides the plate of little round balls covered in powdered sugar onto the table. The aroma makes me drool. "Bike riding. That's healthy of you." She smiles at me. "Nice to meet you . . ."

"Maddie," I supply.

"Maddie," she repeats. "Short for Madeline? I've always loved pretty names for girls." She gives a little laugh then hurries off.

The powdered sugar on the cookies is like first snow. A hard lump lodges in my throat. If I eat a bite, I'll never be able to swallow it.

I'm about to speak when Jasmine says, "I suppose you're going to tell everybody at school about me—about where I live."

"Jasmine, nobody will care." She swings her eyes right into mine. I look away. She wins. Because we both know some kids would care.

"Are you clueless or lying? It has to be one of the two."

"Okay," I concede. "Some idiots might care."

Jasmine stares up at a corner of the ceiling.

"But there's nothing wrong with living here. As far as I'm concerned."

"Thanks for your stamp of approval. But how would you know, Maddie?"

I'm not going to cry in front of her. "Okay, you're right. I don't know what it feels like to live here. Okay? I just want my ring back, Jasmine." I reach into my pocket. "Here." Her ring clatters on the table, wobbling until it stops.

Jasmine stares at me. "We traded."

"You're lying!"

Jasmine's mother appears in the doorway. "Hey! What's happening here?" The kind expression that creased her round blue eyes is gone. Now she looks angry. But not at me.

At Jasmine.

"What did you do?"

Pockets full of stones, shoes of concrete. My mouth opens, but there's nothing left to say. I leap up and storm out the door.

JaSMiNe

The front door shuts. Maddie is too nice to slam it.

"I'll say it one more time. What did you do?"

"Nothing, Mom," I lie.

Mom slumps into a kitchen chair. "Oh, Jasmine, is this Chelsea all over again?"

"No, Mom."

"Then what did that girl want?"

"We traded rings for a while," I say. Glance over to the table and see Dad's turquoise ring there. Breathe in, breathe out. "She wanted me to keep her ring, and she wanted to keep mine." In two strides, I grab the turquoise ring off the table and thrust it onto my finger. It's still warm from being in Maddie's pocket. I hold it out for Mom to see. "She gave it back. But she didn't want to."

Mom grabs my hand roughly, looks at my ring. "But she called you a liar. Why, Jasmine?"

Search my brain for a reason, one that I could tell Mom. "She said I told her all along that the trade was permanent."

"Did you tell her that?" Mom looks intently into my eyes. She thinks if I don't blink it means I'm telling the truth. I don't blink. "No, I never told her the trade was forever."

Mom studies my face a little longer. "Because Dad and I gave this ring to you. A promise to you. That even when Dad left us, his love . . ." She looks out the tiny window, the one with a view of another trailer.

"I know, Mom. I'm sorry." My voice collapses.

"You gave her back her ring?" she asks.

This lie is an easy one. "Yes."

The worst is over. But still I see lines etching into her face. Remember how scared she was driving home. Remember what I promised Dad.

"Hers wasn't as nice as mine," I say. The truth of that rings out.

I wait for an opportunity to look on Mom's phone for Tannis's cell number. Finally, finally, Mom gets in the shower and I tiptoe past the bathroom. Mom's phone is out of power—she must have forgotten to charge it last night. I hunt around her room for her charger, then plug it in. Wait, wait, wait for the red bar to turn green. When it does, I go to her contacts. See "Mike" there right before "Munoz, Tannis." I bite my lip against that sudden pain. Dad's number. Push the pain away and memorize Tannis's number.

I head out to the front porch and text Tannis with my phone.

Tannis, it's Jasmine, I need your help.

Jazz, anything. What's up?

How do I explain? I text: *I'm in trouble.*

Tell me.

I brought a ring to a consignment store. Lady wouldn't sell it and she wouldn't give it back.

Sucks.

Yeah.

Your ring?

Do I tell Tannis the truth? The one person, besides Mom, who actually cares about me? If I don't, I won't be able to look at her. If I do, she'll know I'm a thief. She won't understand why I kept it in the first place. She won't believe how bad I want to give it back.

. . .

. . .

Incoming call. Crap.

Tannis.

"Hello?"

Tannis speaks. "You don't need to tell me the whole story. Believe me, I've made plenty of stupid mistakes myself. And that's all this is, Jazz. A stupid mistake. But there's one person you need to tell. And that's your Mom. . . . Jazz?"

"I'm here."

"And . . . ?"

"You won't go with me to the consignment store to get the ring back?"

Silence.

"Jazz . . . I can't. Your mom . . . she'd be . . . I don't know."

"Never mind," I say. "It was a bad idea asking you for help."

"Jazz."

"It's fine. I'll tell Mom."

"Don't BS me, Jazz."

"I'm not. I gotta go. Okay?"

"Jazz, don't be mad at me. You know I would if I could. I just can't lie to your mom."

Maddie

The September sun sits behind the giant elms. Finally home, I sneak out to the swing set. Maybe Mrs. Sweeney will think I've been in the backyard all this time. When I think it's safe, I trudge inside, a little annoyed that no one noticed I was gone.

To my surprise, both Mom and Dad are out of bed, sitting

at the kitchen table and eating steaming bowls of oatmeal that Mrs. Sweeney prepared for them before she left.

"Oh, honey, you ripped your pants," Mom says.

"That's all you care about," I say. "My pants. You don't care about anything else. Like me. Like if I got hurt."

"Maddie," Dad says, "Apologize."

"I'm sorry, Mom." In that moment, I truly am sorry.

Mom shrugs. "Did you get hurt?"

"No," I say quickly. "I'm fine. Thanks for asking."

"I don't understand, Maddie. Lexi never gets so upset with me. I feel I can do no right with you."

I'm angry all over again. "Why are you always comparing me to Lexi?" I storm out.

I'm sitting at my desk, feeling like a loser for yelling at Mom and Dad, when I hear Lexi scream from her room. "Mom! My ring! It's gone!"

My heart dives to my ankles. Everybody in the house races to Lexi's room. Lexi holds up the velvet jewelry box she keeps on her nightstand. The place for her emerald ring is empty. We are silent, like the inside of a vacuum cleaner before it roars to life or a baby taking a pre-scream breath.

"Oh, Lexi. No." Mom chokes out. "How could you lose Mom's ring?" Mom's voice breaks on the word Mom.

Lexi puts her face into her hands. "I don't know, Mom. I don't know."

Mom turns to Scooter and Pete. "Did one of you take Lexi's ring?"

Pete shakes his head. "No. I don't like rings."

Scooter chimes in, too. "I didn't take her dumb old ring. Rings are for girls. And Dad."

Everyone turns to me. "Maddie, have you seen your sister's ring?"

"I haven't," I say. That's the truth, sort of. I haven't seen it since I gave it to Jasmine. I keep my gaze fixed on Mom, but waves of guilt are pulling me under. I have to tell Mom.

Mom puts her hand to her mouth, as if to hold in words or sobs. She stares down at the floor. She looks up and sighs. "Lexi, I don't have to tell you what this ring means to me." Her face creases in a wry smile. "Plus, I had it appraised last year. It's a $12,000 ring. Edwardian."

Lexi literally wrings her hands. "Mom, I'm so sorry. The last and only time I wore it was my sweet sixteen." Suddenly, Lexi looks up at me. "I remember the way you looked at it that night. You wanted my ring. I bet you took it."

"I did not!" I say hotly. "Maybe you donated it to the homeless."

Mom's eyes narrow. "Did you, Lexi?"

"No," she shrieks. "I *should've* given it to them. They need it more than I do. But I would *never* give up Gram's ring."

Mom turns her hazel eyes to me. She leans in and lightly places one finger under my chin. She searches deep into my eyes and I know I can't look away.

"Maddie," she says quietly, "you've borrowed your sister's things without asking before. I want you to tell me the truth right now. Did you take your sister's ring?" Those last six words she says with the cadence of a trotting horse. Trot, trot, trot. Mom could crack any liar on the witness stand, I've heard Dad say.

Careful to enunciate each word, I say, "No, I did not." Lovely. I've become so good at lying, I've almost convinced myself. I foresee a criminal life. I'll have to flee to Canada. I bet it's cold in Canada. I wonder how long I can survive up there.

Mom's gentle finger drops from my chin. For one loopy moment, I wish she would keep interrogating me. "Hmmm," she says, staring at me and tapping her foot.

"Don't fall for that, Mom," Lexi snorts. "She definitely took my ring. She was bummed that you gave it to me in the first place."

"So? That doesn't mean I took it."

"You did so."

"I did not." I shove her; she shoves me back.

Something falls off a shelf, like the whole house is falling apart along with us. Dad interrupts. "Girls. Stop it. I think what we have to do is search the house. From top to bottom. And Lexi, You have to think hard about what you did when you came home from the sweet sixteen."

Lexi scowls at me. "Fine. I still think she took it, but of course, you don't believe me. I think I took it off that night before I went to bed. The next day, I let Maddie try it on. I tried it on again. I took it off. I went outside and played in the sandbox a little bit with Scooter and Pete."

Dad sighs. "It could have fallen off in the sandbox."

"I said I took it off before then," Lexi reminds him.

"Maybe you thought you did but you didn't."

"We have to dig in there!" Scooter shouts and Pete nods like a little jackhammer. "We have to dig all the sand out."

"Whoa there, buddy," Dad says, grinning. "Okay, let's divide and conquer, shall we? The boys and I will take the sandbox."

Mom says nothing. Her face is squinched up. "Paul," she says stonily. "I don't think you appreciate how serious this is. I don't think you care that my mom's ring is gone."

"You're wrong. I do . . ."

"Don't tell me I'm wrong, Paul." Mom says through gritted teeth.

My mouth opens, but my brain doesn't supply me with any words.

Dad sighs. "Kathy, tell me what to do."

Inside the stretch of silence, I hear Mom swallow. "I'm sorry. I'm really upset. It's just been one thing after another. First the flu. Now the ring. What next?"

"Everything's going to work out fine," Dad holds up his hands like he's under arrest.

Lexi, meanwhile, is on her hands and knees, looking under her bed. "Maddie, why don't you look in your room and the upstairs bathrooms?" Mom says. "Scooter and Pete, you go out with Dad to the sandbox. Lexi, look in here and then go down to the playroom and look in there.

I'll take the kitchen, living room, and the family room."

Dad takes each little kid by the hand. All three of them know better than to look happy about digging in the sandbox at sunset.

My room's a mess of books and discarded clothes. I pretend to look around. All the while my stomach is churning. I'm making everyone waste their Sunday evening looking, when I know we will never find the ring. I keep thinking, "Should I tell?" I picture how angry Mom will be, and how disappointed Dad will be, and how Lexi will be even more perfect, and I will be even more doomed to life in Canada.

We look and look and look. Of course the ring doesn't turn up. Mom does find her favorite pen under her bed, and Scooter and Pete claim that they find buried treasure in the sandbox. But the absence of the ring hangs over us like the scent of burnt toast. Lexi keeps shooting me looks and I keep looking right back at her.

At dinnertime, Dad and Mom are too tired to cook, so we order pizza from Angelina's. I don't feel very hungry but I force myself to eat two slices. Even the twins are quiet—relatively quiet, that is. Scooter uses his pizza crust as a car and zooms it around his plate. That's when I know how upset Mom is—she doesn't bother to tell him not to play with his food.

As we're just finishing up, Pete announces he wants to be a headache for Halloween.

"You can't be a headache, silly," Lexi says.

"How would you be a headache, anyway?" Dad says.

"I paint myself all red," Pete says. "With big lines right here." He points to his forehead.

"Somebody's been watching too much TV," Mom says, coming back to life and ruffling Pete's hair.

"It's my own idea," Pete says.

"I want to be a pirate," Scooter says.

"That's a great idea," Lexi says. She smiles at both boys.

"And very original," I say. "You'll probably be the only pirate in town."

Mom puts down her water glass with a thud and shoots me her warning look.

"Yeah," Scooter says.

"That was sarcasm," I say. "But you're too little to know."

Everyone else ignores me; they've already forgotten how I took care of them while they were sick. It's not fair. If Lexi had been the one to get better first and nurse the family back to health, she'd probably get a presidential medal.

As we clean up, Lexi brings up the ring again. "Mom, I'm sorry."

Mom brushes her hand across her eyes, leaving a few iridescent suds in her eyelashes. Lexi swallows hard. She finishes scraping her plate into the garbage and runs from the room. Rushing from the room is starting to be a McPherson Olympic Event.

"Lexi," Dad calls after her. But she doesn't stop.

What have I done?

Jasmine

The boxwoods planted along Mr. Albert's walkway: dead. The rhododendrons: dead. Cigarette butts scattered around. And near the door: a round black thing, soft on one side. I take one step up the porch, look a little closer, and see the stem. Pumpkin, eleven months old. I stand on the porch, my finger hovering over the bell. Before I can ring it, the door opens.

Ian, wearing a deep blue T-shirt the color of his eyes and jeans, leans into the door frame. I glance over Ian's shoulder—at least I try to—but Ian blocks me. Before he can completely hide the view, I catch a glimpse of dishes stacked up in the sink and a huge pool of ketchup hardened onto a paper plate. The smell of mildewed laundry forces me back a step.

"What are you doing here?" he asks. "Planning to punch me again?"

"You were the one who started that."

"You're lucky you're a girl."

"I could kick your ass if I wanted to."

He laughs. "Oh-kay. Let me repeat: What are you doing here?"

"If there was anyone else to ask, I wouldn't be," I snap. "In fact, this was a stupid idea . . ."

He grabs my arm as I'm turning to leave. "You're here, so why don't you just tell me," he says.

I wrench my arm free.

"Ian," Breanna calls. "You promised."

"Just a minute," he yells back.

"Your minutes take too long!"

"I did something stupid," I say quickly. In as few words as possible, I explain the situation.

He leans against the door. "Well, you've got yourself into a mess, haven't you?" But his voice is kind.

"Can you help me?"

"What do you have in mind?" He grins. All kinds of crooked teeth there, but somehow a nice smile.

I shrug. "I don't know. I thought . . ."

"That I could break into the store?"

"No. Not that. I just . . . I guess I didn't think it through."

We stand staring at each other.

"I could go down there with you . . ."

I sigh. "No, you're right. She'd just say we were two trailer-trash kids."

His eyes narrow. "Is that what she called you?"

"Never mind."

His face changes expressions—anger pinching his mouth, then, when I echo myself—"Just never mind, okay?"—the anger seems to evaporate, and he sighs.

"Ian?" a voice calls. "Is that Mom?"

"No, Bre. Go back to bed."

But she comes out, and when she sees me, her face breaks into a beautiful, gap-toothed smile. "I really knew it was you," she says.

"So you were listening in?" I tap her nose ever so lightly.

Ian scoops her up and she wraps her legs around him.

"Maybe," she concedes. Her brow creases. "What's trailer trash?"

"The garbage in the garbage cans," Ian says without hesitation.

"Will you read me a bedtime story?" Breanna asks me. "Please with sugar on top?"

My eyes find Ian's to know what I should say. He nods, and I follow them inside. Their home is exactly like ours, minus our spiffed-up Goodwill furniture and definitely minus the good smells of Mom's baking and crazy cleaning.

Ian disappears, and I tuck Breanna into her bed, careful not to look on Ian's side of the room. As far as I can tell, she has a single book, one about a purple elephant with pink polka dots. I tell myself that first thing tomorrow morning I'm going to bring her one of my old books—Uncle Louie used to love giving me Disney Pocahontas books, claiming that I look like her.

After I've read the book to her a few times, Breanna falls back asleep. The door makes a soft click when I tiptoe from the room. Ian's waiting for me in the living room, watching a show on mute.

"She's out," I say.

"Thanks."

"I better go."

"Jasmine?"

"Yep?"

"What are you doing after school tomorrow?"

My hand on the door, I turn and grin. "Getting a ring back?"

Monday, September 16

Maddie

At the kitchen table, Dad's hair is smashed on one side of his head and a sheet mark draws a line from his cheek to his chin. I lean down and kiss him goodbye. He pours a spoonful of sugar in the middle of his cereal.

"Really?" he says. "A full"—he glances at the clock—"four minutes before the bus is scheduled to arrive?"

I push the sugar bowl away. "Too much sugar on your Rice Krispies, Daddy-o."

"Oh, no," Dad groans. "You've joined The Dark Side."

"Daddy-o, daddy-o," Scooter chants from the floor, where he and Pete have built a mysterious block world.

"Bye, guys," I say and race out the door, leap off the front porch, and head to North Avenue to wait for my bus with two boys who live across the street from me. They stare at me until I finally say, "I'm Maddie."

The bus pulls up, and I climb on board. I scan the rows for Jasmine, finding her in the very back, sitting with a red-headed boy. The girl she normally sits with is on her own, her eyes glued to a Disney Pocahontas book.

I hesitate, decide that I will wait until we get to school before I tell Jasmine that if she doesn't give me the ring, I'm going to tell Principal Leoni everything—not just the fact that she won't give my ring back, but that I stole it from my sister.

But before Mr. Carty's class, Jasmine is still talking to the red-headed boy from the bus. Their faces are serious, and that more than anything stops me from approaching Jasmine.

"Poetry Café tonight!" Mr. Carty bellows.

I expect to hear a chorus of groans, but instead a buzz of chatter, like a swarm of bees, descends on the room. We spend the period revising, reciting, rehearsing. The kids with the "DD" poems conference with Mr. Carty on their revisions. I sit at my desk, reading Emily Dickinson's biography—trying, at least, but it's hard with Jasmine in the room. After her conference with Mr. Carty, she returns to her desk and writes in her poetry journal without stopping, not for a second, not for anything. When the bell rings, she heads straight for the door. I follow.

"Maddie." Mr. Carty's voice stops me. He motions me toward his desk. "I didn't need to 'DD' your poetry—none of your real work. Just want to remind you that I want to hear something real tonight, okay?"

I have no choice but to nod, but I sort of hate Mr. Carty for outing me. Why does he get to decide who the real me is?

And Jasmine has evaporated. I spend the rest of the day searching for her, but she's not in my classes, or in the lunchroom, or on the bus. And on the ride home, I realize I'm never going to get the ring back from Jasmine, not on my own. I have to tell Mom and Dad the truth. Tell it slant, tell it straight. Tell it.

Jasmine

In Carty's class, Maddie keeps watching me. I know it even though I don't look at her. She's going to stop me after class and talk to me about the ring. The ring I don't have.

As soon as the bell rings, I race out the door, don't look back, drop some papers, don't stop to pick them up. Bang through the front door. Ian will have to understand why I couldn't wait. We talked it through every way, but now I think he can't help me with this. I need to do it myself. Right now.

I am going to that store, getting in that woman's face, taking the ring back. She won't stop me. She can't.

The next time I see Maddie, I'll look at her straight and put the ring in her palm. Maddie's so easy to read and *desperation* is the word I saw all over her face. I remember the way she wrinkled her nose at her algebra problems, the way we laughed so hard we snorted, the way she showed me her room, worried I'd judge her—back when she thought I might be a friend. *I'm sorry, Maddie.*

It's raining. Start walking, then running all the way. Run, walk, run all the way to the antique consignment store.

Closed Mondays.

Maddie

"Welcome to Café Clover!" Mrs. Eilertsen trumpets at the door of the library.

It's strange to be at school at night. On every round table there's a small planter with orange or red mums. The lights are turned off, and instead, Mrs. Eilertsen has placed table lamps around the room. I hardly recognize it as the Clover Middle School library. Except it's teeming with parents. Parents here, parents there, parents, parents everywhere. Kids, too. All three sections of eighth grade.

Mrs. Eilertsen tells Mom and Dad that I'm a "passionate" reader. As a matter of fact, can they please remind me to return *My Mother Is an Alien*? There's a long waiting list.

"No problem," Mom says, glaring at me. Only a preview of the look she's going to give me when she finds out about the ring. If I can tell the truth. I tried to tell them this afternoon, tried more than once. But I couldn't. Standing there, looking into Dad's eyes, imagining his face changing as he realized what I was saying. . . . It was impossible. And when Mom got home, it was even worse.

Before Mom can lecture me about taking responsibility, we run into the Millers, Kate's parents. Our parents cluster by the Junie B. book carousel, chatting away, while Kate and I say hi. And then we don't seem to have anything more to say to each other. It's like a play rehearsal, day one. How do you act like a friend when you're not a friend anymore?

The parents tour the self-portraits. When Dad gets to

my self-portrait and poem, he shoots me a strange look. I shrug. I know, and he knows, that unicorns and rainbows don't really belong in my "I AM" poem. Mom *oohs* and *aahs* over it, of course.

Mrs. Eilertsen shakes a tambourine at the front of the library and tells everyone to take a seat. Mom, Dad, the Millers, Kate, and me scooch into a middle row.

"What's going on with you and Kate?" Mom whispers.

"Nothing."

"Are you upset that she made the team? That's understandable, if you are."

"No, Mom. I'm not. I'm not as good as Kate."

"Sweetie, you're every bit as good as Kate."

"Mom," I anger-whisper back. "Not now. Please."

"Welcome, parents, to Café Clover," Mrs. Eilertsen projects. "Tonight you're going to hear some amazing poetry written by our very own Clover eighth graders."

Mr. Carty joins Mrs. Eilertsen at the front of the room. "Welcome, parents and kids," he echoes. For some reason, he looks nervous in his cool, shiny suit and his skinny tie. "The way this Poetry Café works is: Mrs. Eilertsen will reach into a hat and pull out a name. I'll announce the name, and that student will read one poem."

Three hands go up. Jeremy and his mother, and Mikayla's father.

"Yes?" Mr. Carty says, nodding at them.

"What if you forgot your poetry journal at home?" Jeremy asks.

"I have it," his mother says, waving it around. "But how

does he know which one to read?"

"Mom, I know which one," Jeremy says, flushing.

"Does a poem have to rhyme? Mikayla's doesn't rhyme," Mikayla's dad asks.

"Absolutely not," Mr. Carty and Mrs. Eilertsen say together. Mrs. Eilertsen adds, "But poems can rhyme, too. Rhyming or not rhyming—both work. Any more questions?"

No one has any more questions, so Mrs. Eilertsen reaches into the hat. Please, please, please do not say my name. She pulls out Dani's name.

"Of course," Dani says loudly. "It would be me." At the podium, she looks out at the audience and licks her lips. "This is a poem called 'I Am a Butterfly.'"

She reads:

I am a butterfly flying on a warm summer day.
I am all the colors of the rainbow.
I fly high and I fly low.
I have many friends, also butterflies.
Someday I will have butterfly babies
And we will all live in a beautiful garden.

People clap, and then Sarah takes the stage. Sarah's poem is called "I Am a Puppy." The girls in the front cheer for her.

I am a puppy, golden and sweet.
I like to eat bones and other good treats.

I like to run in the grass
My dad says I'm a nice lass.
Everyone thinks I am awfully cute!
My mom says I'm a beaut!
I love to play with all my friends,
And that is the end.
I hope you like my poem.
Now I'm going home.

We clap and Mr. Carty calls Brendan's name. As he walks by, he glances at me and raises a quick hand.

Just as Brendan is about to begin, the library door squeaks open. Brendan stops. Some people turn around to see who got here late.

Jasmine's shining dark hair is pulled up. She's wearing a plain white sleeveless dress with a slim pink belt and pink ballet flats and her face is scrubbed clean of the lip gloss and mascara she sometimes wears to school.

How could someone who looks so lovely be a thief?

Jasmine

Breanna, holding Mom's hand, pulls her into the room. Ian and I trail after. We picked them up with Ladybug as they were walking down Post Road.

"Sorry we're late," Breanna announces to the people staring at us.

Oh, Breanna. Really?

Mr. Carty, from a million miles away at the front of the room, smiles and says, "Welcome."

We four slide into seats.

Maddie

Mr. Carty says, "Here we have Brendan Cohen, reading 'I Am a Baseball Bat.'"

Everyone laughs.

Brendan coughs into his hand, shoots another glance at me. I smile at him and nod ever so slightly.

I am a baseball bat, strong and proud.
When I hit the ball, it sure sounds loud!
I get up to the plate and pull way back
Strike one! Strike two! Then crack!

Some boys in the audience cheer.

I listen through the whole thing and it's pleasant enough, if you love baseball . . . or Brendan.

"Thanks, Brendan, great job," Mr. Carty says after the clapping ends—Brendan's mom and his dad clap really hard, like they're competing with each other.

Mrs. Eilertsen pulls a scrap of paper from the hat and shows it to Mr. Carty, who says, "All right. Maddie McPherson, please take the stage."

Mom nudges me. "You're on," she whispers.

Gulping air, I grab my poetry journal. I give Mom and Dad a wobbly smile. Scoot past Kate. The walk to the podium takes forever. My breath catches, my heart hammers, and trickles of sweat tickle my sides.

When I get up there, I'm not so afraid after all. I put logic and self-protection in park, and flip to the poem that I wrote one week ago. I changed its ending—my ending—today.

I'm Maddie.
Not my sister, her strong voice echoing
through our house.
Not my brothers, twin halves of a whole,
wrapping their arms around
each other when they sleep at night.
I'm not Dad, funny food man.
Not Mom,
her heart a train that carries her
to work each day.

I'm Maddie, a girl like a story
stuck in the middle.
How will I turn out?
Keep reading.
I'm Maddie, an unmade puzzle,
Put me together.
What's the complete picture?

Maddie, a garden
Seeds planted
What will grow?

"Who am I?" my poem asks.
I don't have all the answers
But if I lie, I know I'm only
a hopeless story,
a jumbled puzzle,
a stunted flower.
If I lie.
about what I love,
about what I borrowed,
about what I regret.

I nod to Mr. Carty, and then I flee to my seat, between Mom and Dad, between a shocked look and a speechless-disappointed-we're-going-to-talk-about-this-later one.

"What lie, Maddie?" Mom whispers, her shoulder against mine, her faded work perfume filling my nostrils like truth serum.

And Dad: His ink-stained fingers thrum his thigh, telegraphing the same message.

Jasmine

Maddie walks to her chair and all eyes are on her. I wish I had the ring in my pocket. Wish I could slip out of this noose. Hate that Maddie doesn't know how much I want to give it back.

The next kid reads a poem about being brave and getting off a ski lift for the first time. Another poem is about achieving a dream of swimming with dolphins. Dozens of poems. Really good poems.

Mrs. Eilertsen reaches into the hat. "Jasmine Princeton," Mr. Carty says.

Ian gives my hand a quick squeeze, one which Mom catches. At the podium, I stare out into the audience. Clear my throat.

"This is from the 'I remember' assignment," I tell Mr. Carty.

He nods, smiles.

My mouth is numb. I close my eyes. I say:

I remember Dad's voice,
his thick black eyebrows, his laugh,
his ridiculously loud sneeze.

I remember Mom and Dad
playing Scrabble and him
letting her win.

I remember Dad singing
"Rocket Man" by Elton John,
making up half the words.
I remember his whistle
that could get our dog Indy
running home
from three backyards away.

I remember Dad and Mom
nursing me through
chicken pox,
trying to keep me from itching.

I don't remember
much of that time
when my dad died
except the sweating rolls
of baloney on platters
at the wake,
the gunshot sound
of Uncle Louie's laugh,
the cracking in
Mom's voice,
calling work to say
she wouldn't be
coming in because
her husband died.

The room is quiet. I see Maddie, her hands covering her heart. I see my own mom's face.

"I'm sorry, Mom," I say after I take my seat.

"Me, too," she whispers back.

Told the truth and Mom's not pissed. She didn't fall to pieces, either.

I'm not sure what she's sorry for, or even what I'm sorry for.

Maddie

I sit in the back seat, staring out the window. All I want to do is think about Jasmine's poem. My theft, my confession, Mom's anger, Dad's anger—it's all out there in the world, something to be ashamed of. But right now I'm stunned by Jasmine's loss. I had the idea she was good at concealing herself, but the death of her dad. . . . Was that why Jasmine and her mom moved to Clover? Was it why she kept my ring?

"How could you, Maddie?" Mom says over her shoulder. "What were you thinking?"

"I'm sorry," I say mechanically. I lift my eyes to the giant beech tree we're passing under. It's been there all my life, and I've taken it—my life, my parents, Lexi and the twins—for granted. As a gift that couldn't be snatched back.

"Sorry? That's all you can say?" Dad whips over to the side of the road, just past the beech, in front of a house already decorated for Halloween.

"Paul," Mom says, reaching over to pat him on the arm.

"She lied to us," he says, as if I'm not there. His voice trembles and from the back seat I can see a muscle jumping in his jaw. "She looked straight into our eyes and she lied."

"I'm sorry," I say again, but this time I mean it. I want to erase the hurt from Dad's voice.

Dad turns and looks at me. He shakes his head. A car drives past, illuminating the back of his head, then the dashboard, and then we're all left again in the dark. "I'll never be able to trust you again, Maddie."

"Paul, you're being too harsh," Mom says. "I'm furious, too. But she's a kid. She made a mistake. That's all."

Dad says nothing, only turns the key in the ignition, puts the blinker on, even though no one is coming, and pulls onto the road.

At home Lexi is busy filling out Amnesty International postcards at the kitchen table. And seeing Lexi, it hits home. I'm in big trouble. Not just with Mom and Dad. But with her.

"How'd it go?" she asks with a smile. "Did anyone figure out a rhyme for 'orange'? Our teacher in sixth grade said whoever came up with a rhyme for 'orange' . . ." She stops, studies my face. I burst into tears, more out of guilt and fear than sadness. "Maddie, what's wrong?"

I slump at the kitchen table, next to her. Mom and Dad take a seat opposite us, a united fence of crossed arms.

"What's going on?" Lexi puts her hand on my arm. "Did somebody boo your poem, Maddie-lu?"

I wish the entire school had booed my poem, because that

would be a thousand times better than what I'm about to tell her. I sit on the hard wood chair, staring at my hands.

"Maddie," Mom prompts.

I look from her face to Dad's. If expressions were weather forecasts, theirs would be stormy with a chance of lightning.

"I took your ring."

Lexi's eyebrows draw together. "You? So, it *was* you?"

"Yeeeees," I wail.

Lexi's mouth drops open. "I knew it." To Mom and Dad, she says, "I told you she did it, and you didn't believe me."

I nod tearfully. "I'm sorry."

"Why'd you do it? Where is it?"

"Shhh. You'll wake the boys," Dad says, half rising out of his chair and sitting down again.

"I was only going to borrow it for a day." My words come out all trembly.

"Borrowing is when you ask, Maddie," Lexi says. "Stealing is when you don't ask. Even eighth-graders know that. Why did you do it?"

"I don't know."

"Well, where is it?"

I explain that I traded with Jasmine, just for a day, and now she won't give it back.

"Are you sure you didn't just give it to her?" Dad asks. "This isn't another lie?"

"No, Dad. I'm not lying."

Again with the hand on his arm, Mom says, "Paul, please."

Lexi glares at me. "Now I'll probably never see it again."

"You'll see it again," Mom says. "Where does this girl live? I'm going over there right now to get it."

"No, you can't do that," I say.

"What do you propose, Maddie?" Mom says quietly.

"I don't know. I wish I could go back in time and not do it. I wish I wasn't even born."

"That's ridiculous," Mom sputters. She rubs the bridge of her nose.

"If it wasn't for me, you'd have the perfect family."

But Dad looks at me closely. "Do you really feel that way?"

"Paul, do you really want her to manipulate you like this?" Mom says in her lawyer voice.

"When Dad thinks I'm a liar, you're on my side. But when Dad's on my side, you hate me again."

"There are no sides," Mom and Dad both say.

"Not for Lexi, maybe. You guys love everything she does. Isn't that why you gave her the ring in the first place? To reward her for being perfect?"

Lexi leans over. I think she's going to hug me, but she suddenly punches me on the arm—hard.

"Ow," I say, grabbing my arm. "What was that for?"

"Yes, Lexi, what *was* that for?" Mom says sharply.

"To show I'm not perfect." She gets up from the table and grabs a vase off it. "Uh-oh. I think I'm going to drop this."

"Alexis Grace." Dad jumps up.

Too late. She smashes the vase to the ground. It's plastic,

but the water and flowers splash all over the floor. She grabs a crystal water glass.

"Lexi. Stop that!" I jump up and snatch her wrist, but I can't keep her from banging the glass down hard, sending a crack through it.

"Alexis Grace, clean this up right now," Mom says ominously, like Mount St. Helens about to blow. We sit there, kind of panting, while Lexi picks up the flowers and wipes up the water.

Lexi *phlumps* down. "I'm supposed to smile and say that's okay when Maddie takes my ring and loses it?"

"Nobody said that," Dad says. "But we do expect you to set a good example."

"I'm tired of setting the example. And guess what? I'm getting a C+ in English."

That shuts Mom and Dad up. They look at each other, dumbfounded.

"Why?" I ask. "You've always gotten straight A's."

"That was before the so-called creative nonfiction unit. That doesn't even make sense. How can it be creative and nonfiction?"

I try not to look happy, but I kind of am. Not that I want my sister to suffer. But I would love to write creative nonfiction. I can't believe there's something I can actually do better than Perfect Lexi.

"Let's get back to the point," Mom says to me in true cross-examination mode. "What do you plan to do to make things right?"

"I guess I should go over to Jasmine's house tomorrow," I say slowly. It's the absolute last thing I want to do after what I heard tonight. She's lost her dad, a dad she loved, just like I love my dad. How could I take a ring away from her? A stupid, stupid ring that I somehow once thought was important.

"Hop in the car," Mom says. "We'll do it now."

"But Mom, it's . . ."

"No buts."

Ten minutes later, we turn in to the mobile home court. Mom wants to walk to the door with me, but I ask her to stay in the car. As I'm about to get out, Mom catches my arm.

"Mom, please, I said I can handle this."

"Maddie, wait. There's something I need to show you." Reaching into the back seat, she hoists up her purse and unzips a side compartment. She pulls out a plastic ziplock bag. Inside is a black leather journal no bigger than my hand. Mom takes my hand and puts the journal in it.

"Dad and I were saving this for your sixteenth birthday, but we thought you should have it now."

Opening it, I know right away what I'm seeing. Gram's strong hand.

You have knit yourself around me, my love
Blue-eyed weave, golden thread
Winter wind whistles through trees,
You against my neck, wool shield.

"Maddie," Mom touches my arm. "Gram was right, I guess."

I look up, blinking hard. "Right?"

"She wanted you to have her poems. That's why Dad and I decided to give Lexi the ring." Mom gives me a half smile, bittersweet. "You know, I'm a bit envious. She was my mother, but she never really shared her poetry with me. And I know what it meant to her."

Closing the little book, I bring it to my face, breathe it in. Open my eyes. "Thank you, Mom."

Then I leave the book on my seat and hurry to the door. Before I can even knock, it opens. Jasmine's mom, her lips pursed, arms folded tightly against her chest, says, "Can I help you?"

I'm having trouble catching my breath. Like a huge wind is blowing in my face. "May I speak to Jasmine?"

"What's this about?"

"I just need to ask her a question."

"And it can't wait for school tomorrow?"

Over her shoulder, I see Jasmine come out of her room. She hurries to the door.

"What do you want?" Jasmine asks.

Don't cry. Do not cry. "Jasmine, I loved your poem." That's not what I was supposed to say.

"You're here to tell me that?" She folds her arms over her chest; the circular scar between her eyebrows contracts.

Okay, I can't do this. I have to do this. "I'm here for my ring."

"I told you, I don't have it. Why can't you leave me alone?"

Suddenly Mom is behind me. "Hi, Mrs. Princeton," she says, extending her hand. "I'm Kathryn McPherson."

Slowly, Jasmine's mom extends her hand. "Nice to meet you. I saw you at the poetry reading."

Mom smiles. "It was great. Uh, Mrs. Princeton . . ."

But before she can speak—before it's Mom to the rescue—I say, "Mrs. Princeton, may I come in? I think that Jasmine and I have a misunderstanding . . . that's all. I just want to talk about it."

Mom glances at me, looks like she's going to say something, but I shoot her a look that says *Don't.*

"Okay," Jasmine's mother says. "Come in."

Jasmine's mom leads us into the kitchen/family room space and points to the two orange butterfly chairs, side by side. They sit on the couch, opposite us.

I can feel the warmth of Mom's body next to mine, and I find it more comforting than I would have guessed. "Mrs. Princeton, I did something bad. I took a ring that belongs to my sister."

Jasmine's mom looks surprised. She looks at Jasmine and then back at me. "Well, we all make mistakes. But . . ."

"Then as if that wasn't stupid and wrong enough, I traded rings with Jasmine. I traded her ring for mine. But when I came here the other day to get my ring back, and to give Jasmine her ring, Jasmine said—"

"Jasmine," her mom says. "Do you have her ring?"

Jasmine

Mom's question hangs in the air between us. I could keep lying, save her from all this worry. I close my eyes so that I don't have to see her face, her eyes searching mine.

"Jas?" Mom's voice isn't going away. This whole mess isn't going away.

I open my eyes, take a deep breath, speak. "I wanted to give it back to you when you first came here. I knew it was wrong even before that. Not giving it back wasn't going to make everything right in my world. It was only going to ruin things for you. I didn't want that, Maddie. Truly. After tonight . . . after I heard you tell the truth in your poem . . . I wanted to give it back even more. But I can't."

"Why can't you?" Maddie asks.

"I brought it to that consignment store by Dunkin' Donuts. The lady took it, and she won't give it back unless I go with a parent." I'm scared to look at Mom—*take care of her, Jas*—but I do. Her hands are fists, her eyes fierce.

"Jasmine," she says. "Why?" But she's not crying.

"I'm sorry, Mom. I wanted to make things better for you, not worse. I wanted to get the ring back and give it to Maddie without you ever having to deal with this."

Mom is nodding, and we've agreed to something without words. She will come with me; she will help me fix this. Her jaw is clenched, a promise.

I feel like a person who's been walking across a frozen pond, like I wasn't sure if I was going to fall through the ice.

"I'll go tomorrow with my mom and get the ring back," I say to Maddie. My head's spinning, my palms sweat.

Maddie looks as miserable as I feel. "I hate the stupid ring," she bursts out. "I'm so sorry about this, Jasmine. I'm sorry about your dad, I'm just . . . sorry."

"Me, too," I say, although I feel a kernel of resentment inside me. This girl is so rich, she has so much. Did she really need to come to a trailer court and wrench a ring out of my hands? I know it's wrong to feel that way, but I can't help it. I do.

"I thought we left these troubles behind in New Hampshire," Mom says, her voice calm, her eyes steady on me. Her hands, rough from cleaning, hold mine tight. A whoosh goes through me, electricity, relief, grief, anger. Ice cracks, and I fall through to another place.

"How can I leave it behind when that's the last place I saw Dad? How can I leave it behind when he's gone and it's not fair? It's not fair, it's not fair, it's not fair."

I'm screaming this. Screaming and crying these words.

Mom pulls me into her arms. I'm crying so hard I can't breathe. Can't breathe. Can't breathe.

Mom says nothing, just holds me and rocks me. Strokes my hair.

"I miss him, Mom. I miss him so much."

"I know you do," she whispers into my ear. "I know you do, sweetheart."

I'm hiccupping and trying to stop crying because somewhere in the room—I'm starting to remember—

Maddie and her mom sit still as cardboard.

And my voice is hoarse and there's snot all over my face and I say, "And how can I leave it behind when you have to work so hard? When everybody else has everything. When people like them . . ." I gesture to Maddie.

Maddie gets up, comes and kneels at my feet. "I'm so sorry, Jasmine. My . . ." She chokes, like this is a sentence she can't finish. Then she whispers, "You're right. It's not fair." Her smile is for me and it is sad. "Jasmine . . ." She bites hard on her lip. "I'm lucky to have my dad, to have so much . . . but . . . my world isn't perfect, not like you think." Her voice just tiptoes out. "You come to school and in two weeks everyone loves you, Jasmine. Everyone thinks you're so pretty and they want to take you skiing and have you sit with them at lunch. I've lived here my whole life and I only have one real friend. Not even one, now."

I sit up, rub the back of my eyes with my sleeve. Maddie's mom hands me a pack of Kleenex. I take a wad and blow my nose. "You think they'd be my friends if they knew I lived in a trailer court?" I ask, not a question but a statement.

Maddie goes back to sit with her mom. "I don't know about them. I only know about me, and I don't care where you live or how you dress. None of that matters to me."

I stare at Maddie, struck by the truth of that. She is oblivious to the things that matter to Sarah and Mikayla and Chelsea back home. I'd thought I could help Maddie by pointing it out to her.

Mom turns to me. "You thought the ring would get us out of the Wishbone?"

"No. But the money could help you pay the bills."

"I'm paying them, sweetie. Little by little." Mom laughs quietly. "You know, I have *always* been the one to pay the bills. Not your dad." She brushes a piece of hair from my eyes.

"Really?" I say skeptically.

"Really," Mom says firmly. "Your dad thought he needed to give you the best of everything. He didn't realize . . ." Mom's voice wobbles a little and my worry rushes back. She clears her throat. "He didn't realize that we had everything we needed."

Mom cups my chin, squeezes one notch beyond comfortable, like she did the morning of my first day at school, like she does when I must listen to what she's telling me. "These bills are not nothing. I won't pretend that, Jas, because you're too smart for that. But I *will* pay them. This is for adults to worry about. For me to worry about, not you."

Then Mom pulls me to her, hugs me tight. "Understand?" she murmurs into my hair

"Yes, Mom," I say, and rest my head on her shoulder, relax into her. Still, she hugs me tight. And I feel her strength, hear it humming in her shoulder.

A WEEK LATER
MONDAY, SEPTEMBER 23

Maddie

It's warm as summer outside even though September is coming to an end and some of the cottonwoods near our school have turned yellow. I step off the bus at school, wanting to talk to Jasmine, but she's already deep in conversation with the red-headed boy—I think his name is Ian. Yes, Ian with Jasmine at the back of the bus; Ian sitting next to her at the Poetry Café. I want to tell her that last night Lexi said she doesn't blame Jasmine for keeping the ring. (She blames me for taking it in the first place, but not Jas; in Lexiland, Jas's reasons = good and Maddie's reasons = bad.)

I'll find a time that's right. Jasmine may be good at holding everything inside, but I'm starting to figure out a few things about her. Lexi's opinion matters to her, even if I think having an older sister is a gigantic pain.

The sky is such a bright blue it makes my eyes ache, so much so that I don't notice Kate standing right in front of me until I almost walk into her.

"Where's Aaliyah?" I blurt.

"We don't spend every second together," Kate snaps.

"Seems like it."

Kate snorts. "C'mon, we gotta hurry. Carty's cracking down."

On the way, I count the lockers to fill up the silence between Kate and me. One two three four. A bunch of sixth graders barrel and bumble toward us. I smile; I remember being that new to middle school, and clueless.

As if we're thinking the same thing, Kate says, "Remember when we were in kindergarten? You used to eat the purple crayons."

"Yeah, because *you* told me they would taste like grape jelly."

Outside Mr. Carty's class, I pause for a moment, but Kate walks on. "Hey, Kate? Are we friends?"

Kate turns back and grins at me. "Duh," she says.

Mr. Carty's standing just inside the door. Kate and I are scooting past when he catches my arm. I boomerang back and stand next to him. "Not so fast, Maddie."

Oh my llama. What did I do? Kate zips to her desk, and I catch her eye. She shrugs.

"Last day of our poetry unit. How about a little poetry reading in class?" Mr. Carty asks. "Maddie, why don't you get us started?"

Before I can give myself time to worry, I reach into my bag, grab my poetry journal. "From the 'I remember' assignment," I explain, though I don't really need to explain:

I remember
The summer before the twins were born
And Lexi was at drama camp
Dad was at a conference
I was eight years old &
Mom said how about you and me
Take a trip to the Cape?
Just the two of us?
We drove for four and a half
Hours and listened to the Beatles
And Mom sang loud!
We stayed at The Sands of Time
And ate clam pizza
On the beach for dinner.
Next day I buried Mom
In sand and kissed
Her nose, we
Swam all the way
Out to the buoys.
We got lost
On the way home
And I promised
Not to tell.
I didn't say
How I wished
We could keep
Getting lost,

Keep singing
"Yellow Submarine,"
Keep sleeping
With sand in our sheets.

The whole class is silent. I wipe my eyes and then I smile. I'm thinking of Gram, how poetry skipped a generation, from her to me. I let myself read one poem from her journal each night. When I get to the end, I'm starting over. Not just because of her words, but because I feel her in the slant of her letters, in the smudge of ink, in her signature. *Here I am,* she seems to say. *Aren't I something?*

Nothing can erase Gram from this world, not so long as I keep reading her poems, and someday, I hope, that will be true for me, too. Someday my granddaughter will keep me alive.

"I love your poem," Jasmine says.

"Raw emotion, people," Mr. Carty says. "The source of poetry."

A beat of silence and then Mikayla speaks into it.

"Mr. Carty?" she says. "Can I read a poem, too?"

He grins. "Absolutely."

All of us hear, but we pretend not to, Sarah's snort of disapproval.

Mikayla grabs her journal and as I'm passing her on my way to my seat, she gives me a high five, like we're on the same team. Fairfield United Poets.

She looks around the room and lets out a long breath.

"I wanted to read this at the Café . . . but I was too scared, I guess." She laughs. "I'm still scared." And she reads:

I used to feel like my life
would gobble me up,
like Jonah was gobbled up
by the whale.

I think it wouldn't be so bad
to be inside a whale
knowing the worst thing
that could_happen already did.

Sometimes I feel like
I'm the whale,
swimming through life
looking for something

that will make me different,
from all the other whales
in the deep blue ocean.

But sometimes
not very often
but sometimes
I'm the ship
sailing

just sailing along.
over the big blue sea
like I know where I'm going
and I know
how to get there.

When she's done, I speak without raising my hand, without being afraid. "Your poem is beautiful, Mikayla."

Other people echo me, even, finally, Sarah.

Jeremy says, "I know how Mikayla feels. I'm like Jonah when I get back a test and I did really bad on it. Then I know that's the worst thing that will have happened for the day. At least I hope."

Robert shouts out, "I'm like an empty whale after school when I'm searching for a snack."

Everyone laughs.

Mr. Carty gazes at us. "Want to know what I think? You're all ships. Heading toward great things."

Jasmine

We're playing soccer today in gym. Maddie rests her hand on my shoulder for balance as she stretches. Brendan walks quickly up to her, talking even before he reaches her. "I brought some Macouns for you," he says. "From apple picking. I'll give them to you after school?"

"That'd be great," Maddie says.

They smile at each other for a second. "Your shoe is untied," he says, then runs off to play soccer.

"He seems pretty nice," I say to Maddie. "Do you like him?"

"Yeah, but my mom doesn't want me to hang out with him until ninth grade."

"That's tough."

Maddie bends down to tie her shoe and from there I hear "Yep." Then she says,

Futile the winds
To a heart in port—
Done with the compass,
Done with the chart.

"Excuse me?"

"Sorry. I just mean my mom can try to keep me away from Brendan, but my heart is in port."

"Thanks for the translation, Poet Girl." I can't keep the laugh from my voice. But it's a kind laugh, and I hope she knows it. Suddenly it's really important to me that she does know it. "I love the fact that you quote poems."

Maddie looks up from her shoe-tying squat and grins. "I'm kind of addicted to Emily Dickinson now. After our GAP report."

Ian hurries onto the field, the baby giraffe. He sees me, too. We wave.

The sun slants into Maddie's eyes as she stands. Squinting,

she holds up her hand. "Do you think your dad would have liked it here?"

I'm about to say no. About to say that the only place he'd ever be happy, and the only place I'd be happy, was Rocky Hill.

But just then the sun shines so recklessly through the autumn leaves, it's like the tree caught on fire.

Like Dad answered for me. A cool northerly wind blows and lifts my hair off my shoulders.

"Yes," I say to Maddie, to Ian and Breanna, to Mom. "He would have loved it here."

The gym teacher blows her whistle, calling us to join the game, and we run.

ACKNOWLEDGMENTS

This novel would not exist without the expert editorial guidance of Rebecca Davis, genius and genie. Thank you for the "DD," the laughs, and the friendship. Blessings for you, Timmy, and Megan.

Thanks also for the insightful editing of the wonderful Cherie Matthews, copyediting of the eagle-eyed Lisa Rosinsky, and marketing of the terrific Kerry McManus.

Thank you, Tina Wexler, super-agent, friend, person I love chatting with on the phone.

Thanks to Sari Bodi, Michaela MacColl, and Karen Swanson, the first line of defense.

Early readers: Lulu Stracher, Sara Zurmuehle, Laura Judd, Allison Schwartz, Sorcha Maddison, Susan Ross, and Samara Cohen—thank you!

Thank you to Patricia Reilly Giff and Suzanne Hoover, my writing teachers, my mentors, and my friends. Also: Sally Judd, Ann and Ali Saberi, Terri Picone, Julie McCoy, Ila Burch, and Linnea Strottmann.

Thank you to my beautiful, intelligent, and deeply

generous sister Kathryn Ann Cummings. I love you, Kathy, and I always will.

Thank you, Aunt Sue, my role model. Thank you, Dad, for a lifetime of kindness and love. Thank you, Rita. You are in every word I write. Thanks to my children, Simon and Lulu, who have put up with a lot of "pasta with a light butter sauce." I love you forever.

Last and most, thanks to Cam, my best friend and love of my life.